Billionaire Unexpected

THE BILLIONAIRE'S OBSESSION

Zak

J. S. SCOTT

Billionaire Unexpected

Edited/Proofed by Faith Williams @ The Atwater Group
Cover Photo by Sara Eirew

ISBN: 979-8-662617-86-5 (Print)
ISBN: 978-1-951102-31-9 (E-Book)

Contents

Prologue

Harlow

Several Months Ago...

"**I** am not leaving you here alone, Taylor!" I said to my intern, with as much force as I could muster. Unfortunately, my mouth was so dry that my voice was little more than an angry whisper.

After nine days of being held captive in a foreign country with no food and very little water, Taylor and I were both starving and critically dehydrated. We'd pretty much burned through any energy reserves we'd had a long time ago. Just trying to speak for any length of time was a major effort.

I glared at the Lanian rebel who had tried to haul me to my feet after cutting the tight bindings on my legs. I'd flatly refused to get up when he'd ordered me to do it. "Take her," I demanded as I nodded my head toward Taylor. "I'll stay."

I didn't speak more than a few words of Lanian, but our captor spoke enough very broken English for me to comprehend that my ransom had been paid, and that they were planning on letting me go.

It was *also* perfectly clear that my intern, Taylor, *wasn't* included in this whole release plan, and that was definitely *not* going to work for me.

"No," the guerilla grunted, and waved his automatic rifle in my face. "You only."

I shook my head.

Not going to happen.

This was *my* geological exploration. I was already missing one member of this small, three-member team. Taylor and I hadn't heard a word about Mark, the third member of our group. He was the mining engineer who had been expected to arrive in this island nation nine days ago to meet up with me and Taylor. I'd spent *every single one* of those nine days frantic about what had happened to him. Not only was Mark a team member, but a man I cared a great deal about as well.

There's no way I'm leaving this damn island until I know what happened to Mark! I have to find out where these assholes are holding him.

Had Mark escaped capture somehow?

Had he been abducted, too, but had already been released?

Or was he barely hanging on like Taylor and I were doing right now?

Not knowing his fate had been eating me alive since the day Taylor and I had been kidnapped at gunpoint moments after our arrival in Lania.

"You come," the rebel insisted in an angry voice as he bumped the barrel of his assault rifle against my head.

I shook my head again.

Maybe I *should* be terrified, but the adrenaline necessary to feel that emotion had been drained from my body through deprivation and emotional intimidation.

All that I had left was…resignation.

I *was* going to find Mark.

I *wasn't* leaving my intern here to die alone.

There was no energy left for fear anymore.

I didn't *want* to die, but if the bastard did end up shooting me, he'd have no choice but to let Taylor go if he *had* to release a hostage. The man let out a savage snarl, and stormed out the door of our small prison. I cringed as I heard the grating sound of metal on metal as he secured the barricades on the door. It was a foreboding noise that always reminded me of just how precarious our situation was at the moment, and how little time Taylor and I had left.

The small room had gone dark as soon as the door was closed, and the momentary reprieve we'd gotten from the stifling heat while the door was open ended abruptly.

There was almost no ventilation in the one-room structure where we were being held, and very little light got through the minuscule windows near the ceiling. Hell, could I really call those *holes* "windows"? Taylor and I could barely get our hand through them, and they provided very little air movement to negate the oppressive heat of Lania in the summer.

"You have to go, Harlow," Taylor said in a scratchy, barely audible voice. "You know you do. If you don't, Mark and I will probably die before we're rescued."

I let out a small groan as I lowered my upper body to the dirt floor next to Taylor, feeling completely spent just from the effort of sitting up for a few minutes.

Dammit! I hated myself for getting Taylor involved in this situation at all. Mark and I were both employees of Montgomery Mining, and had been for years. Granted, I was a research geoscientist now, so I didn't do a lot of field work anymore, but it wasn't like Mark and I weren't experienced with explorations.

Taylor Delaney was simply a summer intern working under my guidance at the Montgomery Mining Lab in San Diego. Honestly, she wouldn't even be here in Lania if I hadn't made the fateful decision to let her come along on this expedition. Taylor had just finished her master's degree at Stanford, and I'd thought her studies in environmental geology would be helpful.

Yeah. Okay. I'd also *wanted* her to come so she could get her first experience with international field work, too. I was supposed to be her mentor, so I wanted her to get every single opportunity possible during her internship that would help her in her future career.

However, if I'd thought for even a single second that bringing Taylor along would put her life in danger, she never would have set foot in this damn country. She wasn't *just* my intern. Taylor and I were friends, too.

How could I have ever imagined we'd end up in this situation?

Nothing about this routine trip should have been dangerous. There wasn't supposed to be any political unrest in Lania anymore, and it should have been perfectly safe for her to be here with me.

"How can I do that, Taylor?" I rasped. "How can I go and leave you and Mark here?"

"How can you not?" she countered weakly. "If you don't go and try to get us rescued, none of us will last much longer."

"Don't say that," I pleaded, even though I knew she was right.

Taylor and I were both extremely debilitated. We hadn't eaten in nine days, and the small amount of rainwater we'd been gathering through the tiny windows was drying up. Periods of rain were short and sporadic here. We'd gotten to the point where we'd go through long periods of silence because we simply didn't have the energy to speak anymore. More and more often, we were having periods when we weren't completely lucid.

Eventually, our bodies would give up the fight. We'd fall asleep, and just never wake up again.

"We're realists, Harlow," Taylor answered softly. "We both know we've been slowly dying of dehydration for days now. I'm not sure what kind of shape Mark is in at the moment, but I'm sure time is critical for him, too. The rebel will come back. Let him get you out of here so *you* can get Mark and me out of here, too. Once you're back in the States, you can tell the negotiators what's really happening here. I know you'll raise hell until someone comes for us."

"I want them to take *you*," I whispered. "I don't want to leave you here. I'd rather be the one who stays."

"You know I love you for that, but it's not going to happen," Taylor answered. "I'll be okay, Harlow. If I know you're on your way home, it will give me some hope. Something to live for if I know help is coming."

My heart rebelled at the idea of leaving Lania without Taylor and Mark, but my brain knew she was right. "I don't understand why you're not being released with me. If my ransom was really paid, it must have been Montgomery Mining that paid it. The only one who would care enough to fork over money for me is my mom, and she doesn't have that kind of cash."

"And you think Montgomery would have paid for the release of a mere intern, too?" Taylor murmured.

"Yes. I know they would have. The Montgomery brothers are billionaires, but they've always made sure they ran a fair and ethical business, even though it's the largest mining corporation on the planet. I've worked for them long enough to know that they *do care* about their employees, even their summer interns." I'd once been one of those summer interns myself, so I knew they were good to every employee, and not just their upper corporate management.

"Then maybe the rebels only agreed to releasing you first so they could get more money," Taylor suggested. "There's definitely nobody out there who would hand over the kind of money they're probably demanding if Montgomery doesn't do it. Nobody will ever even know I'm missing."

"I'm sure it has something to do with the money," I agreed. "And your *friends* would know you're missing."

"You're the only friend I have in San Diego, and the only person who even knows I'm here," she whispered.

Since Taylor had recently relocated to San Diego to do her summer internship, I couldn't argue with her about that statement. Her college friends from Stanford were probably spread out around the country by now, and Taylor had no family.

I desperately wanted to reach out to Taylor to comfort her, but I couldn't. Our hands were tied too tightly for me to wrap an arm around her to give her a hug.

The fact that I'd been helpless to do a damn thing to help Taylor had slowly torn me apart. Her safety had been my responsibility, and I'd completely let her down. "We'll get through this, Taylor."

Even as I said those words to comfort her, there was no real conviction in my statement.

Without food.

Without more water.

Without some kind of break from the suffocating heat in this small holding cell, Taylor and I would probably be dead within a day or two.

I bit back a groan as I felt some circulation starting to return to my legs.

I was almost used to the pain of them being bound so tightly that every muscle in my legs was begging for relief.

Now that they were finally free, I realized that my previously decreased circulation had probably dulled some of the pain of the abuse.

"Taylor?" I queried softly. "You still with me?"

Damn! It was sad that I needed confirmation that she was still breathing.

"I'm here," she rasped. "Please don't worry about me, Harlow. Go get us some help. I'll stay right here dreaming about a big pitcher of ice water until I get rescued, too."

"And a big, juicy steak with a loaded baked potato," I answered automatically.

Taylor and I had made a game out of discussing the first things we wanted to eat and drink once we escaped from this hellhole. I knew *that* particular meal was number one on her list.

"I know how hard this is for you, Harlow," Taylor murmured. "I wouldn't want to leave you behind, either. But it's our only chance. Nobody back home knows that we aren't getting any food, and not enough water to sustain life for any length of time. Maybe they think taking this whole rescue slow and safe is the best way to handle it."

"I'll go," I reassured her. Even though I knew it was my only option, the decision was tearing my heart from my chest. "You're right. Whoever is negotiating our releases has to understand that they're running out of time."

"They're back," Taylor mumbled as the annoying, high-pitched sound of the door being unlocked sent a shiver of dread down my spine.

"I'm going," I said breathlessly. "I'll get you out of here as fast as I can. Don't give up, Taylor. Please, don't give up. Just hold on for a little while longer."

"I'll do my best not to die on you, Harlow," she promised. "We've made it this long. I think I can survive for another few days."

Sunlight flooded the room as the rebels shoved the door open. I was so unaccustomed to bright light after nine days of almost constant dimness or total darkness that I closed my eyes, and then blinked hard until my vision adjusted.

The guerilla had brought reinforcements, and this time, I couldn't fight it when three of them yanked me to my feet.

"Dammit!" I cursed, doing everything I could do to stay upright as pain tore through my left knee.

I knew the injury was more than just atrophied and strained muscles from being bound for so long. I'd twisted my knee when the rebels had first kidnapped us and slammed Taylor and me to the ground.

Yeah, it hurt, but really, a knee injury had been the least of my worries.

Until now.

I needed that damn leg to walk out of here.

My heart ached as I glanced back at Taylor, and saw how fragile my normally happy, redheaded friend looked right now.

If I didn't *know* it was Taylor, I may not have recognized her at all.

"You go," one of the rebels said as he pushed me toward the door.

I stumbled, and lost sight of my friend.

I have to keep my focus on my objective right now. I have to be strong for Taylor and Mark.

I let go of an anguished sob as I limped unsteadily out the door.

Maybe I needed some kind of temporary release, but I wasn't about to break down completely.

I had one single-minded purpose, one goal, and the only thing that would be able to keep me from accomplishing it was death.

Since it didn't look like today was my day to die, I was determined that Taylor and Mark wouldn't spend one second longer in this shithole than absolutely necessary.

Chapter 1

Harlow

The Present...

"I don't need a Last Hope *advisor*, Marshall," I said to the older man who was sitting across from me at my kitchen table. "Especially not one like Jaxton Montgomery, for God's sake. You know what I want. I'd desperately like to be part of Last Hope instead of being treated like one of their rescues."

Marshall took a sip from his coffee mug and raised his brow.

It was a look meant to intimidate most people, and God, I had to admit that the former Commander Marshall had one hell of a don't-even-try-to-argue-with-me presence.

However, *those* expressions that were meant to alarm anyone who saw them didn't work on *me* anymore.

Maybe he'd been the supreme leader to every man who had served under his command on his Navy SEAL team. I also had no doubt he'd deserved that hero-worship, too. But there was so much more to Marshall than just his former military career. Over the last few months, I'd seen a *different* side of Marshall that I was sure he didn't really want *anyone* to see.

Not that he'd become a teddy bear or anything even close to warm or affectionate, but he wasn't the complete hard-ass that he wanted everybody to think he was, either.

"You know the rules," Marshall said gruffly. "Anyone involved in Last Hope is former Special Forces. No offense, Harlow, but you're in no shape to tackle *someone else's* kidnapping right now. Not when you haven't even dealt with your own issues from being a captive yourself. That's why I made Jax Montgomery your advisor. You have work to do on those issues, missy, and it would help if you had someone to talk to who can actually help you work through them. Have you even bothered to answer Jax's phone calls?"

I rolled my eyes. I hated it when he talked to me like he was my father. "Jax dropped by earlier today," I admitted.

"Let me guess. You blew him off," Marshall said knowingly.

I shrugged. "I told him if he could go two weeks without being photographed with one of his one-night women, then I'd agree to let him be my advisor. It was the easiest way I could think of to get rid of him, and never have to see him again. I doubt he'll last a single day without being pictured with yet another female. He's been a playboy for years. That's the last thing I need right now."

"He's also one of the two men who risked their lives to rescue Taylor," he reminded me.

I sighed. He was right. Jax and Hudson Montgomery hadn't hesitated to put one of their private jets in the air as soon as they'd discovered that Taylor was in bad shape.

In fact, by the time I'd hunted them down at their corporate offices after my release, Marshall, Jax, and Hudson had already been planning to execute a rescue for Mark and Taylor.

One thing I hadn't realized when I'd left Lania was the chance of Taylor ever being released by paid ransom was almost zero. Apparently, Lanian rebels were known for taking the ransom money for the last hostages to be released, and then killing every one of them. An attempted rescue had been the *only* option for her.

I had to admit, I was shocked when I discovered that all three of the Montgomery brothers were members of a secret, volunteer rescue operation called Last Hope. Marshall had started it after he'd retired from the Navy due to an injury. Jax, Hudson, and Cooper Montgomery had jumped on board years ago, after they'd all left their Special Forces units.

Not only were they active members of Last Hope, but I suspected they were financing the operation as well. From what I'd seen, Last Hope was way too sophisticated to be a volunteer group on a shoe-string budget.

"I know," I confessed shakily. "And nobody will ever be more grateful than I am that they got to Taylor in time. It's not like Jax and Hudson *had* to do the rescue themselves, but because they did, they saved Taylor's life." God, not even in my wildest dreams could I have imagined that the powerful billionaires who owned the company I worked for were part of a highly secret, civilian organization like Last Hope.

If Jax and Hudson *hadn't* been part of Last Hope, and highly qualified to execute their own rescue immediately, Taylor never would have made it. Had they wasted *any* time putting together another team of guys, I was fairly certain they would have been returning Taylor to the US in a body bag. Neither Taylor nor Marshall had ever told me *exactly* what shape she'd been in when she'd been found. But I wasn't a total idiot. I knew she hadn't got up and walked out of there on her own.

Desperate, Taylor had made a feeble attempt at escape once I'd left the compound, and she'd been severely beaten for her actions.

I couldn't blame her for trying to self-rescue when she'd had the chance. I probably would have done the same thing, but the punishment she'd gotten for that offense had just weakened her condition even more.

I had no doubt if Jax and Hudson hadn't gotten to her in record time, there would have been no way to save her.

Last Hope, and the advanced capabilities of the operation, had managed to pull off what had seemed like an impossible rescue.

Marshall had contacted Crown Prince Niklaos, the current ruler of Lania, and arranged for basic medical care for Taylor before Hudson and Jax even left the dock in Lania. Taylor had gotten the life-saving IV fluids and basic medical care necessary to keep her alive on the long flight back home.

I had no idea how Marshall had formed any of his connections in high places. What normal person knew the Crown Prince of Lania?

Marshall fixed his dark-eyed stare on me as he asked, "Why *wouldn't* they be part of Last Hope? Before Hudson, Jax, and Cooper came back to San Diego to take over Montgomery Mining, every one of them were damn good Special Forces officers."

I shook my head. "I guess it just doesn't make sense. Most billionaires don't go into the military in the first place, so I guess the whole idea of them being part of a secret, volunteer, private rescue operation doesn't fit, either."

Marshall shot me a disappointed look. "I never took you for the type of woman who judged a man by how much money he had," he grumbled. "Your mom isn't like that, and she definitely raised you right, so I'm a little surprised."

"You barely know my mother," I protested.

Sure, Marshall had come to Carlsbad to visit me while I'd been recovering at my mom's house, but that hardly made him an expert on my mother.

Unless…

"Are you two still communicating?" I asked suspiciously, and immediately got a nonverbal answer when he averted his gaze. "I knew it. I knew you had a thing for my mother."

Marshall cleared his throat. "I don't have *a thing* for your mother. We're friends. And yes, we still talk occasionally, but that's *all* we do. She's way too attractive to be interested in a man who can barely walk," he said in a disgruntled voice. "And stop avoiding my question, Harlow."

Seriously? Marshall was far from disabled. Yes, he had a pronounced limp from the injury that had ended his career in the Navy SEALs, but he was still an attractive man.

"I'm *not* judging Jax and Hudson because of their *net worth,* Marshall. I was just saying that them being part of Last Hope was... unexpected," I explained. "What employee would ever imagine that their three billionaire bosses rescued hostages in foreign countries in their spare time?"

Marshall leaned back in his chair. "Maybe it is unusual, but the Montgomery brothers are a unique group that I'm damn happy to have on my side. So tell me what you have against Jax Montgomery, other than the fact that he dates, and is never photographed with the same woman twice. You seem to like Hudson, and I've never heard you say a bad word about Cooper."

"I've actually never met Cooper," I confessed. "And how could I *not* like Hudson? He makes it very obvious that Taylor is the center of his world now, and he's making her incredibly happy. Plus, *he's* never been a man-whore. In fact, I don't think I've ever read a single word of gossip about *him* or Cooper."

Hudson, the eldest Montgomery brother, had taken care of Taylor while she was recovering, and the two of them had fallen madly in love. They were living together in an exclusive relationship now, and Hudson had convinced Taylor to take a permanent position as a geologist at the Montgomery Mining Lab.

There was no way I *couldn't* adore the man for giving Taylor all the happiness she very much deserved.

"They're *all* good men, Harlow, whether you've realized that yet or not," Marshall rumbled.

I took a sip of my coffee before I answered. "Jax Montgomery asked me out on a date once about two years ago. He visits the lab sometimes because he's interested in the research, and after we met there, he asked me out for dinner."

I hadn't really wanted to share that information, but if I wanted into Last Hope, I couldn't evade Marshall's questions.

"And?" Marshall prompted.

"And I told him that I wasn't interested in being one of his one-night women. The press follows him everywhere when he's in the company of any female just so they can report on his latest rejects. I would have to be an idiot to sign up for that," I informed him.

He shrugged. "Most women would just because he comes from a very well-known family, and because he's so wealthy. The women he's dated seem to love the attention they get from being seen with him."

Unfortunately, I knew Marshall was right. There never seemed to be any shortage of females willing to take a shot at being the first to get a second date with Jax Montgomery. "He is filthy rich," I admitted. "And he's obscenely gorgeous. But I wonder how many of those women actually know that the guy is literally a genius, too. He's wickedly intelligent. It's almost embarrassing that I have a doctorate degree, but Jax seems to be able to keep up on geoscience discussions in the lab as well as I do."

Not that I'd actually talked to him much *after* I'd refused his dinner invitation. I'd seen him around the lab, but we'd actually never had a long discussion after that. In fact, I'd made it a habit to avoid him whenever possible.

Marshall smirked. "You do realize that he *will* end up being your advisor, right? Jax has a stubborn streak a mile wide, so I guarantee you won't see a hint of gossip about him because of your agreement. It's not like he squires a different woman around *every single night*. You've underestimated him, Harlow. If Jax makes a deal, he sticks to it."

I lifted a brow. "He also said he wouldn't date another woman for as long as he was my advisor so he was always available if I needed him."

Marshall nodded. "Then he won't date. For some reason, being your advisor is important to him. *He* came to *me* about it. It's not like I approached him. I've never asked a single one of the Montgomery brothers to act as an advisor. They're too damn busy."

"He did?" I asked, surprised. "Why would he do that?"

Jax hadn't said a single word about the fact that he'd actually *volunteered* to be my Last Hope advisor.

"Maybe because he can see how much you're struggling right now, just like I do," Marshall said grimly. "You resigned from a job you loved, and you barely leave this tiny apartment of yours, Harlow. I know you've been occasionally seeing a counselor who *you* chose, but I think she's just blowing smoke up your ass. You need somebody who can help you confront your demons, not help you run away from them. I don't think you've even thought about forgiving yourself for bringing Taylor on that expedition, and I know you're still grieving Mark's death. I have no doubt you're blaming yourself for that, too, which makes absolutely no sense. At some point, you're going to have to figure out that it wasn't your fault. That *none of it* was your fault."

"I can't," I responded in a shaky voice. "Taylor being in Lania *was* my fault, and I *invited* Mark on that exploration. If it hadn't been for me, Mark wouldn't have been there, either, and he never would have been executed by rebels when he arrived in Lania."

I'd been completely shattered when Marshall had broken the news that they'd recovered Mark's body near the dock, and that he'd been dead since the day that Taylor and I had been locked up as hostages.

Apparently, the Lanian rebels preferred to dispose of the males, and keep only the women as their prisoners. The bastards obviously assumed that a female would put up less resistance.

"None of it was your fault, Harlow," Marshall said adamantly. "All of you were *victims*. Nothing you did was out of the ordinary, and Lania isn't exactly hostile territory. There was no way you could have predicted that this could happen. Taylor has already moved on, and she and Hudson are incredibly happy. Have you two discussed what happened to her after you were ransomed out? I think it's important for you to actually realize that Taylor has done her fight with her demons, and came out of that struggle a winner."

I shook my head. "I think she's been trying to protect me by not talking about it. I still believe she was sexually assaulted, too, but she doesn't go there, either. Honestly, I don't think I *ever* believed her explanation that she was taken out of our holding area every night to speak with the rebel leader about our release. God, maybe I just *wanted* to believe that because I was so frantic about Mark, but even when it was happening, it didn't make sense."

"I think you should talk to Taylor about it. She's doing far better than you're imagining," Marshall suggested. "And even if it *did* happen, and you *had* known, what could you have done about it, Harlow? You were as powerless as Taylor was at the time, so there was no possible way you could have helped her. Not to mention the fact that you didn't have an assault rifle handy." He paused for a moment before he added, "I'm sorry about Mark. I know you two were dating. Were you in love with him?"

I swiped a tear from my cheek before I answered. "I think we were both still trying to figure things out. His job as a mining engineer kept him out of the country most of the time, so we were rarely able to actually go on a real date. We spent a lot of time talking on the phone or FaceTiming. That's why I suggested he join me on the exploration. He was between jobs, so I thought it would give us a little more time together in person. I wasn't in love with him, and I don't think he was in love with me, either. We didn't really have enough time together to find out if we *could* be right for each other. But he was a good man, and an amazing friend. I cared about him a lot."

"A loss is a loss," Marshall observed. "I guess it doesn't really matter if you two had it all figured out or not. I know you miss him."

I nodded. "I do. I miss his voice and talking to him almost every day."

Mark had always been so upbeat and supportive. The two of us connecting to share what was happening in our lives had become one of the best parts of my day.

"I know you do," Marshall said solemnly. "And I'll be the last one to tell you when and how you should grieve that loss. But you have to let go of all the guilt, Harlow. It's eating you alive. If Mark was the man you say he was, he wouldn't want you to be walking around like a zombie the rest of your life."

I blinked back the tears that were threatening to fall. I knew that Mark wouldn't have wanted me to shoulder the blame, but I couldn't stop myself from feeling like his death was my fault.

"Maybe I could stop obsessing over what happened if you'd let me get involved in Last Hope," I muttered. "I get that you have to keep tabs on anyone who finds out about your organization. I also know that you stay in contact with your victims because you want to help them through the recovery process. But I *wasn't* one of your rescues, Marshall. I was ransomed out. Right now, I really need to feel like I'm part of something important. Something that means something. I don't want to just be a victim who needs to be assisted by Last Hope. I want to be actively involved as a volunteer."

"Harlow," he said in a warning voice.

I held up a hand. "Don't. Please don't give me the rules again. Maybe I wasn't in Special Forces, but I *was* six years active duty in the Air Force, which I'm sure you already know."

I had no doubt my mom had told him how I'd managed to get through school, or he'd already found out by other means.

Marshall was pretty scary when it came to information gathering, and he made it a point to know as much as possible about anyone who knew about Last Hope.

Maybe Hudson and Jax hadn't rescued me, but I'd been treated like one of their victims since the moment Hudson had been forced to tell me about how they were going to rescue Taylor.

I took a deep breath before I added, "I was a weather specialist in the Air Force, Marshall. That could be a really valuable skill. I'm not asking you to send me into recovery situations. I know that isn't an area where I can help you. I don't have that kind of training. But maybe it's time for you to consider utilizing support people. I already know about Last Hope, so it's not like you'd have to tell someone about it who doesn't already know. And I've kept your existence a secret, just like you asked. Who's doing your weather research for your missions right now?"

"Unfortunately, that would be me," he grumbled. "Last Hope isn't hurting for funds. I have all the newfangled equipment. I just haven't completely mastered it yet."

I folded my arms over my chest. "So you're pretty much a jack-of-all-trades in this organization?"

"When I don't have the Special Forces volunteers with the skills I need, yes," he snapped, sounding frustrated.

I let out an exasperated breath. "You can't learn those skills overnight. It takes schooling and a lengthy on-the-job training period before you can be proficient at it. Take me on, and I can give you weather analysis and predictions anywhere, even in space. I had to have a secret security clearance for that job, Marshall. We were the ones who analyzed weather for military missions."

"Harlow, you aren't ready—"

"I'll do whatever you want," I interrupted breathlessly. "I'll work with your recommended counselors, and see if they can help me. If Jax comes through on his promise, I'll let him be my advisor. Just don't say no. I'm not used to being idle all day, Marshall. I'd be happy to help you organize the equipment you need and set it all up the way it should be."

Yeah, I knew I sounded desperate, but I *needed* some kind of purpose in my life right now.

"All I want is for you to get your life back, Harlow. I doubt you could even make it to the headquarters with the kind of anxiety you're experiencing at the moment," Marshall answered. "I don't want you to try to use Last Hope as some kind of distraction, either."

"I'm not—"

"You are," he told me flatly. "But I'm willing to make you a deal. Work with one of the best counselors we can recommend who specializes in this kind of trauma. Also, I want you to work with Jax as your advisor. And that doesn't mean just going through the motions with him. Really work with him and follow his suggestions. We have advisors for a reason, Harlow. You need someone you can turn to after this kind of emotional trauma. It's not just going to go away on its own. You should know that by now. You've gotten worse instead of better."

I opened my mouth to argue, and then closed it again. I could hardly tell Marshall that everything he was saying wasn't true.

He continued. "If everything goes well, and Jax tells me that you're making significant improvement, I'll seriously consider letting you be our first support volunteer if that's still what you want. Honestly, you might be right. Last Hope has grown a lot, and we could use some skilled volunteers who aren't necessarily physically involved in rescues. I'm grateful that many of our former victims who have recovered stepped up to help other victims in an advisor role. It takes a lot of the load off my guys. We also have medical and psychological professionals who have a limited amount of information about what we do. We think of them more as sympathizers than volunteers, and not a single one of them has outed us yet. I guess we've never considered trying to recruit people who know about Last Hope to officially be part of our team of volunteers."

I was slightly deflated because he obviously wasn't going to take me up on my offer anytime soon. "How long—"

"As long as it takes," he said firmly. "If I decide to take this step, I want to know you're signing up for Last Hope because it's really what you want. Being part of this organization isn't an easy gig, and I'd have to have you healthy in mind, body, and spirit."

I sighed. "I understand." Maybe I didn't like it, but I knew he was right.

If I wanted him to take me seriously, I needed to have my head on straight.

He stood up. "Good. We've always been here for you, Harlow. All you've ever really needed to do was let us help you. I think you'll be surprised at how quickly things change with the right treatment."

It wasn't like I didn't know that Last Hope was there for me. Marshall had made it a point to check up on me at least once a week, and it wasn't like he *had* to do it himself. He could have very easily given up on me since I'd refused a regular advisor and any of their recommended professionals. I didn't know just how big Last Hope really was, or how far of a reach they had, but I was aware that he probably had any number of people who could have done these simple check-ins for him.

I got up as he limped past my chair. "Thank you, Marshall," I said softly and impulsively kissed him on the cheek.

This man had been one of the most constant, reliable people in my life over the last several months.

"No need to get all sappy on me, missy," he said, sounding slightly embarrassed. "It's all part of the job."

I rolled my eyes. *None* of what Marshall did was *a job*, and he certainly didn't get paid for it. He did it because the man had more conviction in a single day about doing what was right than most people would ever feel in a lifetime.

I followed him to the door, but he turned before he departed and nodded toward my leg. "You need more treatment on that knee. Obviously, the physical therapy you had in Carlsbad didn't cut it. Being inactive allows that healing knee to stay weak."

Yeah, my knee *was* bothering me, but... "How did you know?"

"I'm a man who's lived with a leg injury for years now," he answered drily. "I pick up the subtleties."

"Please don't tell Mom about any of this," I pleaded. "She worries."

He shot me a sympathetic glance. "You've done a damn good job of convincing your mother that you're okay, Harlow. I'm not about to crush her illusions, but I will make sure that those illusions become a reality. You deserve a hell of a lot better than this."

I didn't have a chance to respond before Marshall walked out the door.

I sighed as I closed the door behind him, wishing I could believe that I was entitled to anything better than the life I was living right now, too.

Chapter 2

Jax

"Why in the hell didn't you tell me that you had a romantic interest in Harlow Lewis?" Marshall asked irritably the moment I walked into his office.

"Nice to see you, too, Commander," I answered drily. "Could you at least give me a chance to sit down before we start this inquisition?"

I was stalling because I hadn't quite seen *that* question coming.

Maybe I should have been prepared for *something* unusual. Marshall's request that I stop by his office sometime this week wasn't exactly normal. Usually, Hudson, Cooper, and I all met up with Marshall when we had Last Hope business to discuss.

"Cut the sarcasm and just answer my question," Marshall demanded.

I dropped into the comfortable chair near his desk. "Does it really matter? I asked her out one time two years ago, Marshall. She turned me down flat. End of story."

He shot me a dubious look. "Is that the end of the story? Why did you really come to me about being Harlow's advisor, Jax? And don't bullshit me. There's always a reason for doing something out of the ordinary, and you've never showed any interest in being an advisor in the past."

I had way too much respect for Marshall not to try to answer as honestly as possible. "I'm not exactly sure why I did it," I confessed. "I've been following Harlow's progress since she was released as a hostage, and she's not doing well, Marshall. She's had very little counseling, and she's been refusing to talk to an advisor. When I saw her last week to try to convince her to let *me* be her advisor, she still looked like she'd been dragged through hell and back. Whatever she's been doing, it's obviously not working."

Marshal nodded sharply. "You're right. She's not well, and she needs someone to turn to right now who has her best interests at heart. I trust you. Always have, Jax. But I want to know that you're going into this advisor role for the right reasons. She has refused every time I've offered her an advisor. I need one who won't take *no* for an answer, and who will stick to her like glue and not give up on her."

"I want to help her," I replied shortly. "Isn't that reason enough?"

"You still attracted to her?" Marshall asked suspiciously.

Okay, so *that* was a tricky and somewhat uncomfortable question for me.

I wasn't sure there would ever be a day when Dr. Harlow Lewis wouldn't get my dick hard whenever I saw her, but I knew it was more than lust that had made me volunteer. I didn't have a problem getting laid, and I wasn't a *total* prick. Even though I was physically attracted to her, there was no fucking way I would be hitting on a woman when she was as low as Harlow was right now.

I cleared my throat. "She's a beautiful, highly intelligent, blue-eyed, blonde female, Marshall. Is that really a fair question? There aren't many guys who *wouldn't* find her attractive. But I didn't offer to help her just because I wouldn't mind fucking her. I hope you know me better than that."

"I do," he said gruffly. "I just wanted to know what your motives were when you offered to be her advisor. It's not exactly comforting that you're not sure why you're doing it yourself. But just the fact that you've noticed that she desperately needs help is good enough for me. However, I do wish you would have shared that you had a history with her."

"We don't have any *history*," I scoffed. "Honestly, other than the fact that I *did* ask her to have dinner with me a long time ago, I hardly know her. Most of what I know about Harlow is through her work in the lab. The woman gets completely obsessed about her projects. She's motivated. She's curious. She's driven to find the solutions to problems no one else has even noticed yet. Her behavior isn't normal right now. She looks like she no longer gives a fuck about much of anything. It doesn't take a genius to figure out that whatever treatment she's getting isn't working."

"I don't think she's sleeping much," Marshall shared unhappily. "I think she's probably having nightmares, even though she hasn't mentioned it. Harlow has finally agreed to see one of the psychologists who *we* recommend, so I set her up with Dr. Romero. She's one of the best in the field for post-trauma anxiety and stress."

"Agreed," I said, surprised that Marshall knew so much about what was happening with her right now. "Are you still in contact with Harlow?"

"Never stopped making contact with her," he answered. "I was the only one from Last Hope who she'd trust enough to let through her door. She needed someone, Jax. Her mother would be extremely supportive, but Harlow doesn't want to tell her that she's anything other than completely healed. Besides, it's not like she can tell her mother all about Last Hope, so I thought it was a good idea for me to keep checking on her."

I nodded. Nobody knew about Last Hope unless it was absolutely necessary that we tell them, and our rescues were asked never to out us. Luckily, none of them ever had…yet.

There wasn't a single volunteer for Last Hope who didn't know that we could end up being front-page news someday, and that the publicity would make it hell for us to fly under the radar. For the most part, we didn't dwell on that possibility. We'd deal with it when and if it happened.

"So if her mom doesn't know about Last Hope, who does she think *you* are?" I asked curiously.

"I keep it vague," Marshall replied. "She assumed I was some kind of government employee assigned to help Harlow after what happened. I've never disputed that assumption."

I grinned, knowing Marshall was probably a lot more comfortable in *that* role than one of the usual made-up identities we used as advisors. "You didn't want to pretend to be Harlow's latest love interest?"

"Hell, no," he grumbled. "I'm old enough to be her damn father."

"Probably just barely," I mused.

None of us knew exactly how old Marshall was, but my best guess was early to mid-fifties. Even though I trusted and respected him completely, he wasn't exactly the kind of guy who spilled much personal information about himself.

"I'm old enough," Marshall responded in a clipped voice. He was quiet for a minute before he spoke in a more solemn tone. "I guess I've let Harlow's situation get to me. I like her, and I like her mother. It's not like I, of all people, don't know better than to get personally involved with a rescue, but I fucking hate what's happening to her. She busted her ass to get through all those college degrees of hers, and it doesn't seem fair that one incident made her throw it all away. Granted, it *was* a horrific hostage experience, but her mom told me that working for Montgomery as a research geoscientist has been Harlow's goal since high school. What in the hell is she supposed to do now that she quit her dream job?"

I gaped at him, trying to reconcile the red-faced, obviously agitated man in front of me with the Marshall who could generally run an entire mission without ever raising his voice or breaking a sweat. Hell, I didn't think I'd *ever* heard him put that many curse words into a single statement, either.

This was a side of Last Hope's fearless leader that I'd never seen before, but fuck knew I understood *why* he was upset. It was hell watching an exceptional woman like Harlow get completely destroyed by something she didn't deserve and that she'd had zero control over.

"Maybe we aren't *supposed* to get personally involved, but we're also human, Marshall," I said gravely. "The entire situation was fucked up. All three of them were completely innocent victims who were just trying to do their jobs. To be completely honest, it's rattled the whole Montgomery organization, including me and my brothers. Hell, look at Hudson. I don't think anybody could get more personally involved than he did, and we all feel guilty because they were in Lania for Montgomery. We cleared that exploration as safe, and it wasn't." I paused for a moment before I added, "And just so you know, Harlow is *still* a research geoscientist for Montgomery, and I plan on making sure it stays that way. She's just on a leave of absence right now."

Marshall's eyes widened. "She said she resigned."

I shrugged. "She tried. We didn't accept her resignation. Do you really think we're stupid enough to let a talented geoscientist like her leave and eventually go to the competition? When I follow through on my promises and become her advisor in another week or so, and that *will* happen, she agreed to stay on leave until she could consider her decision to resign with a clearer head. Hell, none of us wants her to leave. Harlow's done some incredible work for us, and we want her to keep on doing it. The only reason she tried to quit is because she's too damn willing to take responsibility for everything that happened."

Marshall nodded. "She feels guilty because of what happened to Taylor. She thinks she made a bad call taking an intern with her to Lania. And she feels guilty about Mark, too, because she invited him and arranged for him to be on her team."

"He probably would have ended up assigned there anyway," I grumbled. "He was one of the few engineers who was free to go that week. None of this was *her* fault. No one saw this coming, not even the Crown Prince of Lania. If *they* had no intel that a small group of crazies were hiding out in an isolated area of their country, it sure as hell wasn't on anyone else's radar. Nobody could have foreseen this happening. Harlow, Taylor, and Mark were just in the wrong place at the wrong time."

"Yeah, well, try convincing Harlow of that. She's not thinking rationally," Marshall said irritably.

"That's not surprising considering what she's been through. I think you and I both know how easy it is to start blaming ourselves when we lose a friend," I answered. "I'm glad you got her set up with Dr. Romero. She gets really quick results. I think if Harlow had started out with her, she'd be doing as well as Taylor is right now."

"She's stubborn," Marshall replied in a disgruntled tone. "She wanted to do things her way, and she didn't really trust Last Hope in the beginning. It's ironic that the only thing she really wants now is to be a Last Hope volunteer."

I raised a brow. "Seriously?"

Marshall released an exasperated breath. "Oh, she's completely serious, but I'm not sure that Harlow isn't looking for something to use as a distraction. I told her I'd consider it if you decide she's made significant improvement at some point in the future."

I listened as he went on to explain Harlow's history, and exactly what she wanted to do for Last Hope.

"I can't say it's a bad idea," I mused. "I had no idea she was former military, but now that I do know, it makes sense. I can see it in the work she's done at Montgomery. All of her reports and notes are extremely organized, and the way she researches is very disciplined. Hell, I thought she was just anal compared to some of our other researchers, and her attention to detail is actually an asset for Montgomery."

"I think it's just part of her personality, too," Marshall told me. "According to her mother, Harlow was always a very disciplined overachiever."

"I'm not sure that's necessarily a good thing," I informed him. "Overachievers have a very hard time cutting themselves any slack."

Marshall looked at me curiously. "You speaking from personal experience?"

I shrugged. "Maybe."

After growing up with dysfunctional parents like mine, it was hard *not* to be an overachiever.

Marshal shook his head. "I have no idea how your advisor relationship with Harlow is going to turn out, but it will be interesting to watch. I'm not sure which one of you is more bullheaded."

"Me," I assured him.

I have absolutely no intention of giving up on Harlow Lewis, no matter how obstinate she is about trying to shake me off.

He smirked. "You're probably right. You did give up dating and women to help Harlow while you're her advisor, which is pretty extreme."

Shit! Apparently, Harlow hadn't left out any of the details of our agreement.

I crossed my arms over my chest. "Why does everybody make such a big deal out of that? It's not like I'll die without a damn date. When I was a SEAL, there were times I didn't even see a single female for months at a time."

Recently, for some unknown reason, I'd had zero interest in dating at all, but he didn't need to know that. Knowing Marshall, he'd dig at me until he knew why, and I didn't have the answer to that question.

Marshall cleared his throat. "I think you gained your reputation because you've never been photographed with the same woman twice. It seems to me that the media makes such a big deal out of your one-and-done dating habits that every time you do it again, the reporters lose their minds."

"I guess I've never really cared what they thought," I grumbled.

"Can you really blame Harlow for turning down your offer to take her out?" he asked earnestly. "Maybe *you* didn't care what the media thought, but *she* obviously did, and you know those reporters would have made her life hell for at least a week or two. Or until they had a new target."

"It was definitely an ego-damaging experience," I responded, trying to make light of the whole incident. "I'm not holding a grudge, if that's what you're asking. Well, no more than any guy would who had a woman laugh in his face when he asked for a date. Honestly, that particular day might have been the *only* time I actually regretted my reputation."

Whether it was true or not, I preferred to think that Harlow would have said *yes* if it hadn't been for my reputation as a player. She'd seemed perfectly comfortable discussing her research with me. It was only *after* that dinner invitation that she started looking at me like I was a lunatic.

Looking back, maybe I shouldn't have just impulsively blurted out that dinner offer in the middle of our business discussion.

Even now, I wasn't quite sure how it happened.

I'd never been that asshole boss who hit on every attractive Montgomery employee. In fact, my brothers and I made it a point *not* to date employees, and we took any sexual harassment complaints within the company very seriously.

In the end, I'd chalked my unusual behavior up to a moment of temporary insanity, even though I'd never had one of those episodes before or since that day.

Yeah, Hudson had fallen off the never-date-an-employee wagon after he'd met Taylor. However, my older brother could hardly say he'd only lost his mind temporarily. When it came to Taylor, Hudson was completely deranged all the time.

"Your ego obviously recovered," Marshall drawled. "Don't screw this one up, Jax. I think Harlow really needs you, and I'm going to turn all of her advisor responsibilities over to you."

"I don't plan on failing," I assured him. "Just brief me on what you know, and I'll take it from here."

I wasn't sure if Harlow really needed *me*. In fact, I was almost certain that she'd prefer to never see my face again.

Nevertheless, she could definitely use a friend and advisor who understood what she was going through. So, like it or not, Dr. Harlow Lewis was just going to have to get used to me being a huge pain in her ass in the very near future.

Strangely, I suddenly realized just how much I was actually looking forward to that.

Chapter 3

Harlow

"What are *you* doing here?" I asked as I answered the door. Squinting from the bright sunlight, I gaped at Jax Montgomery, who was leaning against the doorjamb like he'd been waiting forever for me to open the door.

"Are you okay?" he questioned. "I rang the doorbell eight times before you answered."

"Um…yeah. I was just taking a nap. It's not like I *knew* you were coming here unannounced," I finished defensively.

If I'd known it was Jax Montgomery ringing the doorbell, I probably wouldn't have answered. This isn't exactly the way I want to admit that he won.

I raked a hand through my hair as I continued to stare at him, knowing I was a total mess. I hadn't slept well the night before, so I'd fallen asleep on the couch. It *was* possible that he had rung the doorbell quite a few times before I'd finally woken up.

I sent him my best withering glance of displeasure, but all he did was grin back at me.

God, it was incredibly unfair that a guy with Jax's wealth and success was *also* one of the most gorgeous men I'd ever laid eyes on.

I couldn't see the compelling green eyes that I knew were hidden beneath a pair of dark sunglasses, but every other attractive feature he possessed was on full display.

He kept his brownish hair short, probably just a little longer than it had been in the military. Obviously, he spent a lot of time in the California sun, because he had some lighter highlights in his hair that looked completely natural.

Even dressed casually in a pair of stonewashed jeans and a yellow T-shirt with some kind of surfing logo on it, Jax Montgomery was breathtakingly handsome. The way those everyday clothes hugged one very tall, muscular, droolworthy body was enough to make any woman stare.

Yeah, beautiful men were everywhere in Southern California, but it wasn't just his hard body and his perfect features that made him so attractive.

Maybe it was his intelligence.

Maybe it was his confidence that bordered on cockiness.

Maybe it was the fact that he seemed to exude an overwhelming amount of male hormones.

Hell, I didn't know what it was that made my heart trip every time I saw Jax Montgomery, but there was *something* about him that made the man almost irresistible.

He grinned a little wider as he looked at his watch. "I'm actually late. It's been two weeks, twelve minutes, and about…fourteen seconds since we made our agreement."

"Did you come here to gloat?" I asked as I ran a self-conscious hand through my unruly hair again. Maybe I didn't like him, but it was almost impossible *not* to feel a little embarrassed when my hot boss showed up at my door, and I *knew* I looked like crap. "Okay, you won. Are you happy? I didn't plan on being a sore loser. I was going to call you."

As soon as I was ready, which might have taken a day…or three.

He shook his head. "I didn't drop by to brag about winning," he said earnestly. "I just wanted to see you. Can I come in?"

I reluctantly opened the door wider. He obviously wasn't going away, so I might as well deal with him now. "My place is kind of a disaster. I haven't had a chance to pick up."

So, that statement wasn't *quite* accurate. The truth was, I hadn't been motivated enough to care about picking up, and keeping my small apartment as tidy as I normally did. Admittedly, that wasn't something I really wanted to share with Jax. My complete lack of interest in anything made me feel like a total slug.

As he entered, I hurriedly ran around my small living room and picked up a couple of used coffee mugs. I quickly straightened up the couch pillows and tossed the throw blanket over the back of the couch before I went into the kitchen.

"It's fine, Harlow. I came to see you, not your apartment," he drawled. "And I brought a friend I want you to meet."

Oh, God!

I turned, and met Jax's mesmerizing gaze. He'd ditched his sunglasses, and I could see a hint of mischief in his gorgeous eyes.

I looked away from him to frantically search for the visitor, expecting to be mortified because someone I didn't know had followed him into the apartment.

My eyes moved from Jax to the unknown guest, and the tension suddenly drained from my body.

His friend wasn't a "who."

It was more of a "what"—in canine form.

My heart melted as I met the most earnest pair of circular brown eyes I'd ever seen peeking out from a very furry face.

I dropped to my knees and petted the adorable dog. "Oh, my God. What a cute dog. Is this a girl or a boy?"

"Her name is Molly. She's a Lhasa apso, and she's one of the smartest dogs I've ever helped train. I thought you could use some company for a while. But she's just on loan. Her owner will want her back, eventually."

I smiled as I sat, and Molly moved into my lap, licked my face, and then made herself comfortable on top of my crossed legs.

I ran my hand over her silky coat as I asked, "Don't Lhasa apso dogs usually have really long coats?"

"Usually," he agreed. "But Molly isn't a show dog, and it's too damn hot here to make her wear a fur coat like that."

"Not that she isn't adorable just the way she is," I assured him. "She almost looks like a puppy."

"She's five, and most Lhasas look like puppies forever with a shorter haircut."

"She's so sweet. Who's her owner?"

"Me," he answered with humor in his voice. "And my golden retriever, Tango, will go into perpetual mourning if I don't bring his buddy back at some point." He motioned to the canine. "Molly. Come."

I was slightly sad when the pup immediately went to Jax's side.

"Down," he instructed.

Molly laid down instantly.

"Wait," he said calmly.

The dog put her head down on her front legs like she was perfectly content to stay exactly where she was right now.

"She's such a good girl," I said in a slightly awed tone as I got to my feet. "Did you really help train her?"

He nodded. "I've been working with an organization that trains service dogs for veterans with PTSD for several years now. Molly was the one dog I just couldn't give up after her training, but I can lend her out for emergencies when somebody needs her."

Okay, I was surprised. I'd *definitely* never pegged Jax as a dog lover, or the kind of guy who donated his time to help train them. Most likely, he supported this organization financially as well if the program was something he believed in that strongly.

I went into the kitchen, found a clean coffee mug, and started making myself a cup of coffee. "I've heard about a few of those programs. Is it helping our military vets?" I asked curiously.

"Definitely," Jax replied. "We can tailor a dog's training for different levels of PTSD. Sometimes all they need is an emotional support dog, and sometimes they need a dog with a higher level of training to be a service dog."

"So what's the difference between the two?" I questioned.

I finished making my coffee, and then brewed another for Jax when he confirmed that he wanted one. While he was waiting, he explained how the program worked, and how they trained different types of dogs.

By the time he was done, I had to give the guy kudos. It sounded like his heart really *was* into helping veterans.

"So what got you interested in this program?" I asked as I gave him his coffee and we went to sit in my living room.

The space seemed much too small as Jax lowered his powerful body into my recliner, and I sat on the couch.

He called Molly into the living room. "Do you want her to sit with you?" he asked.

I nodded.

"Just call her up to you," he instructed.

"Molly, come," I said tentatively.

Without any further instruction, the dog happily leaped onto the couch and settled herself right beside me with her head in my lap.

"Good girl," I crooned as I stroked her silky head.

"I got involved because I believe in the program," Jax said, finally answering my question. "I don't think I ever realized how much some of the things I saw on a few of my missions affected me until I was actually out of the military. Maybe once the adrenaline wasn't constantly pumping, I finally noticed how hypervigilant I was, even when I didn't have to be. I started having some occasional flashbacks, and I went through several months of not sleeping more than a few hours because of recurrent nightmares. When I signed on with Last Hope, Marshall saw a few of the signs, and he pushed me to go see a good therapist for PTSD, and recommended I get myself a pet." He took a sip of his coffee and swallowed before he added, "I'm not sure which one helped more, the therapy or the dog, but having that constant canine companion did help. Dogs don't judge. They accept you exactly as you are as long as you're good to them."

I automatically opened my mouth to respond, but Jax had stunned me into silence. I took a very slow sip of my coffee to wrap my mind around what he'd just said.

I guess I'd never expected Jax to just throw out the fact that he'd suffered from some PTSD after getting out of Special Forces. I knew that the elite military group had a high number of guys who suffered from it, and there wasn't a single shameful thing about admitting that. In fact, my respect for him as a person had just multiplied because he could so easily talk about something that must have made him pretty vulnerable at the time.

I swallowed hard as I realized that Jax was laying out his past experience to make *me* more at ease. He wanted me to know that he'd been there, done that, and survived it.

He wants me to feel comfortable talking to him. That's why he shared.

My heart melted just a little as he shot me an earnest green-eyed gaze.

Suddenly, I knew *exactly* why he put his time and effort into helping other veterans suffering with PTSD. He'd been through it himself, and he wanted to help others with the same issues. Since I was a veteran myself, that touched me more than I wanted to admit.

It would have been easier for a rich, successful guy like Jax to put it behind him and never think about what had happened to him again once he'd resolved his issues.

The fact that he hadn't, and was willing to talk about it so freely had taken me by surprise.

I finally nodded. "Thank you for what you're doing. I was active duty Air Force for six years, but I never saw combat. I never even had to leave the country. I guess I was lucky because my MOS felt more like a technical job."

Jax shook his head. "Marshall told me, and don't downplay the importance of your support role in missions. What you did was important, Harlow, whether you worked in a combat zone or not."

I shot him a weak smile. "Thanks. I kind of miss the comradery sometimes. Maybe that's why I want to help out with Last Hope. Did Marshall tell you I offered my weather specialist services?"

"He did," Jax said cautiously. "And I'm not against the idea because we could use that help, but we can't even consider it until you get your head on straight, Harlow. We have to have every team member strong, no matter what their role is in Last Hope," he said bluntly.

My first instinct was to tell Jax that I was fine, but I knew I wasn't. "I want to be that person again, but I'm not sure I can be," I told him in a shaky voice. I was so tired of trying to hide the way I felt that I kept talking. "I can't pretend like it didn't happen. I can't make the nightmares go away. I can't get rid of the fear of being out in the open, where something could happen all over again. I hate the fact that fear and guilt have made me a completely different woman than I was before this happened, but I can't change it. God, after what happened to Mark and Taylor, I don't know if I have the right to be any happier than I am right now."

"Hell, yes, you do!" Jax said gruffly. "Don't let a bunch of asshole rebels continue to run your life. If you do, *they* fucking win."

I startled as Molly pawed at my leg, stood up, and nudged my face with her snout.

I reached out to stroke her head. "What?" I asked her in a softer voice.

"She can sense your distress," Jax explained. "She's trying to make sure you're okay."

"I'm okay, girl," I cooed as I stroked her body and patted the space next to me. "Down."

Apparently satisfied, Molly plopped back down beside me.

"Look at me, Harlow," Jax demanded.

I looked up, and our gazes locked.

For some reason, I was comforted by the unwavering certainty in his eyes.

"You *will* get through this," he said calmly. "One step at a time. I know what happened to you messed with your head, and you may never be exactly the same woman you used to be. Hell, we're defined by our life experiences, but this won't change who you are, Harlow. I promise it won't, and I'll be with you every step of the way until you tell me to fuck off because you don't need me around anymore. You got that?"

Feeling mesmerized, I nodded slowly. "I'm scared, Jax," I confessed. "I've never been depressed or unreasonably fearful. I'm not even a functional or useful human being anymore."

"Yes, you are. You're just not seeing who you are right now. Just consider this the downtime that you need to regroup, and for fuck's sake, cut yourself some slack. I get that you feel guilty about Mark and Taylor, but neither of those things were *your* fault. I hate the fact that as your employer, I sent you into that goddamn country in the first place. I could easily take the blame for what happened to every single one of you in Lania, but that shit would eat me alive. The truth is, it wasn't *anybody's* fault, Harlow. It was a random incident that nobody could have predicted. You got that?"

"I'm not sure—"

"No. Fuck the uncertainty, Harlow. Tell me you got that, because if you don't, I'll sit right here and tell you that a million times until you internalize it. If it wasn't my damn fault, then it wasn't yours either, right? Think about it, Harlow, and use that brilliant reasoning ability I know that you have inside that intelligent brain of yours. Do you think *I'm* to blame because I was the asshole who sent you to Lania in the first place?"

Jax *wasn't* to blame, nor were *any* of the Montgomery brothers. It was a routine exploration to a country that was known to be safe. "Of course I don't think it's your fault," I said softly. "You couldn't have known what would happen. It would be like expecting you to be psychic and predict all of the mass shootings in this country or something similar."

He lifted a brow as he continued to hold my gaze. "If you can process *that* truth, then why in the hell are you blaming *yourself*? You couldn't have known what would happen, either. You made your decisions based on the fact that Lania was perfectly safe for international travel, which was true. Montgomery sent you there with that same assumption. There was nothing wrong with any of the decisions you made. Taking Taylor to Lania, and inviting Mark to join your team were both perfectly reasonable things to do. Now, tell me you got that."

My mind started to spin.

If I really reached for sanity and reason, what he was saying made sense.

"Harlow," he said in a persuasive baritone.

Tears started to pour down my cheeks as I slowly nodded. I was panting with emotional turmoil as I finally said, "Rationally, I know you're right, but I'm not sure I can turn off the negative thoughts in my head."

"Hold on to your reason as often as you can," he suggested. "Once you manage to internalize the truth, everything will change. It won't happen overnight, Harlow, but it will happen once you can change those thought patterns. Keep telling yourself that it isn't your fault over and over, and keep reminding yourself that you don't have the power to predict random incidents that never should have happened. Nobody does. Not even the all-powerful co-CEOs of Montgomery Mining, and there's very little we *can't* do."

I let out a startled laugh as I realized that he was actually mocking himself and Montgomery with his pseudo arrogance.

I swiped the tears from my face as I muttered, "God knows I'm not nearly as powerful as any of the Montgomery brothers."

Jax winked at me mischievously. "Glad we got that straight. Now let's go for a walk. Molly could probably use a short outing."

And just like that…I went from feeling a little better to complete panic mode in a matter of seconds.

Chapter 4

Jax

T he moment I saw the panic on Harlow's face, I felt like a
complete asshole.

Christ! Maybe I should take back the walk suggestion, and
tell her we don't *have* to leave her apartment right now.

Yeah, I had some experience in dealing with post-traumatic stress,
but I wasn't a damn therapist. I was flying by the seat of my pants
with nothing to really guide me except instinct and my own previous struggles.

My intuition was telling me to get her outside and into the fresh
air, even though it looked like that was going to be a major hurdle
for Harlow.

She'd self-isolated for so long that every fear she had was now
about a hundred times bigger than they had been right after the
kidnapping.

I got my ass up and walked over to the couch. "Hey, I'll have your
back, Harlow," I assured her. I lifted my shirt to show her that I
was carrying a 9mm in an inside-the-waistband holster. Hopefully,
knowing I was armed would be a relief rather than a trigger for her.

Hell, I was ready to do almost anything to convince her that she'd be safe stepping outside with me. "It's just a short walk. I was a SEAL who got my ass shot at on a fairly regular basis. I think I can manage to protect you if we go for a short walk."

Her apartment building was small by San Diego standards, and it was somewhat neglected inside and out. The appliances, décor, and exterior were outdated, but it was in the Balboa Park area, so the neighborhood was pretty decent.

When she looked up at me, the mixture of longing and fear in her beautiful blue eyes tore me up.

I held out my hand, hoping to hell I wasn't pushing too hard.

Oh, hell no, I am not going to start doubting my instincts right now just because Harlow looks so damn fragile and exhausted.

It was my responsibility to help her get her damn life back, even if she was reluctant to take those first steps.

I felt like a goddamn hero when she took my hand and let me pull her to her feet. "I'm scared, Jax," she said quietly.

"The first time is always going to be the hardest, Harlow," I told her calmly. "It will all be downhill after that."

Molly jumped off the couch and sat beside me with barely contained excitement as she waited to see what was going to happen.

Harlow ran a nervous hand through her hair. "I'm a mess. I should probably change—"

"You're fine," I interrupted, cutting off any protests she was going to start making. The jeans and lightweight pink shirt she was wearing worked just fine since it had been somewhere around eighty degrees outside the last time I looked. "We're not going far. Just put your shoes on."

The last thing I wanted to do was prolong the agony and indecision for her right now, but I still had to ask, "Do you need a compression bandage on that knee?"

"Do I even need to wonder how you knew about that?" she grumbled as she put her feet into a pair of black, casual slip-ons near the door. "And no, I'll be fine without one."

She needed gentle exercise to strengthen her knee, and she probably would be okay without the extra support for a short, easy distance. Once we got to the point where we were doing anything more strenuous, I'd wrap that knee up myself if necessary. "Marshall did brief me about anything that he thought would help," I confessed as I clipped on Molly's leash. "We're both concerned that your knee never completely healed."

I held out the end of the leash to Harlow, and she took it reluctantly.

"These the keys?" I asked as I swept up a set from the side table, along with my sunglasses and a pair I assumed were Harlow's.

Since the only items on the keychain were a keyless control for her car, and a single key, it didn't take a genius to figure out which one went into the apartment door.

Harlow nodded nervously.

Jesus! How long had it been since the woman had been outside? She looked terrified.

I yanked the door open and motioned her out. "Ladies first."

Molly started forward, but Harlow didn't move.

When the canine sensed Harlow's fear, Molly gave her a sharp bark of encouragement.

"She's trying to tell you it's safe to go out," I told her patiently. "If she sees something she doesn't like, or if she has bad vibes about somebody, you'd know it."

Harlow shook her head like she was snapping out of her internal thoughts, and cautiously stepped outside.

Feeling like I'd just conquered the fucking world, I handed Harlow her shades and locked the door before I dropped the keys into my pocket.

I couldn't see her eyes because she'd put on her sunglasses, but I could feel the tension in the air as she turned her head to look at the closed door of the apartment.

Oh, hell no, don't even think about it, beautiful. We're full speed ahead and no turning back now.

I took her hand and gently pulled her forward. Luckily, she was in a ground-floor apartment, so there was nothing else we had to do but walk. "Let's stop in the parking lot so I can grab a poop bag from the car just in case."

I could see Harlow's throat move as she swallowed hard, and then she nodded. "Okay," she answered in a barely audible voice. "Hopefully, she'll do her thing really quickly. About the only thing that got me out that door was knowing you have a gun and most likely know how to use it."

"If the need to shoot someone should suddenly arise, I won't miss," I informed her drily.

I wasn't about to tell Harlow that when Molly was in unfamiliar territory, she often felt the need to take a piss in several different places before her bladder was completely drained. My girl liked to spread her scent around, and that could make this a longer walk.

A quick glance at the tension in Harlow's face told me that now wasn't the time to share that information. It was likely to cause her to drop the leash and make a run for her apartment.

"Tell me about the Air Force," I suggested, eager to keep her talking to take her mind off her own thoughts.

"There's not much to tell," she answered with a shrug. "I went in right after high school and served a six-year enlistment. My dad died when I was a sophomore in high school. Things were tight at home, so I knew I was going to have to get creative. I didn't want to be completely buried in student loans once I finished college. I got as many college courses as possible knocked out while I was enlisted with tuition assistance, and I was able to use the GI Bill once I got out. The training also got me a higher-paying civilian job after I was discharged, which helped a lot while I was doing my master's program."

"I know what happened after that," I told her. "You did a summer internship with us, and got offered a full-time position at Montgomery once you were finished."

It was pretty rare for Montgomery to hire a summer intern, but Harlow had been one of the few exceptions because she'd done such great work during her internship.

She nodded. "I was really lucky. Montgomery has such good tuition assistance programs that I hardly had to take on any student debt to finish my doctorate."

I could tell that she was starting to relax because her speech was a lot more natural than it had been when we'd left her apartment. "It wasn't luck, Harlow. It was hard work. You played your military gig perfectly to get the most out of what they offer for college assistance. Plus, you picked a technical field with specialized training that would help you get a good job when you got out. I don't think there are that many high schoolers who are mature enough to plot exactly the right way to graduate with a doctorate without being buried in student debt."

"They do if they can't afford to get a doctorate any other way," she said, and then stopped abruptly.

I watched as she lifted her shades and stared at my vehicle. "What in the hell is *that*? I know it has to be yours because I doubt any of my neighbors can afford a Ferrari."

I grinned as I opened the car door to grab a plastic baggie from the glove compartment. "It's not *just* a Ferrari," I informed her. "This is a 599 GTO. I've had her for years, and she's still one of my favorites."

Harlow let out a small groan as she dropped her shades back over her eyes. "Please don't tell me that you're a sports car crazy kind of guy. I was just starting to like you. A little."

I had to force myself not to laugh as I closed and locked the door of the rare black Ferrari, and started walking toward the sidewalk. I kept a strong grip on Harlow's hand just in case she decided she wanted to bolt. "What's wrong with appreciating the mechanics of a really nice, high-performance vehicle?"

"Oh, God, you *are* a car crazy guy," she said, sounding disappointed. "Vehicles serve a purpose. They should be functional. They're supposed to take you from point A to point B, hopefully with decent gas mileage. I guess I don't see the point of owning a fancy Italian sports car that costs more than some people's houses."

I stopped myself from pointing out that the price of *that* particular Ferrari cost more than *most* people's houses. There was no point in giving her more ammunition to use.

"Then you've obviously never gone from zero to sixty in less than three seconds," I drawled in a teasing voice.

Honestly, I'd never met a woman who was completely unimpressed with my vehicles, and I found Harlow's ultra-practical reaction completely fascinating.

She let out a huff. "Yeah, so that's kind of my point. The thrill is over in less than three seconds, and then you're stuck with a car that's extremely overpriced, noisy, and a major gas hog."

I chuckled. "Sweetheart, zero to sixty in less than three seconds *never* gets old."

She snorted as she stopped for a moment to let Molly do a urine drop. "I can't help but compare it to riding the same roller coaster over and over. At some point, the initial thrill has to wear off."

"It hasn't for me," I told her honestly.

"At least you hang onto cars longer than you do girlfriends," she mumbled.

A second later, she inhaled sharply. "Oh, God, I shouldn't have said *that*. I'm sorry. You've been incredibly nice to me today, and that was a bitchy thing to say. Your dating preferences and vehicle choices are really none of my business."

I wanted to tell her that she could criticize my taste in women and cars all day long if it helped chill her out, which it obviously did.

I gently propelled her forward with a small tug until we were walking down the street in front of her apartment building. The foot traffic was fairly minimal since it wasn't a main thoroughfare.

"Did you really think I was going to be offended?" I asked, amused. "It's nothing I haven't heard thousands of times. Even my own brothers razz me about my dating habits."

"They're your brothers. I'm just some woman who's lost her mind who you're trying to help," she said remorsefully.

"You're *not* crazy, Harlow," I told her firmly. "You went through emotional and physical trauma that most people will never understand because they'll never experience anything like it. I think your sleep deprivation is intensifying your anxiety to the point where you don't even want to deal with going outside anymore. You think that if something like that could happen once, it could happen again. Plus, you have a knee injury that never quite healed, and that's just one more vulnerability that you don't need right now. How am I doing so far?"

"You're doing so well it's kind of scary," she replied with a small sigh. "I'm always exhausted, but most of the time, I don't want to fall asleep because of the nightmares. Sometimes I dream about things that really happened, like flashbacks. Other times, I dream about Mark getting executed or the rebel leader hurting Taylor, stuff that I didn't really see. It seems like the dreams just keep getting darker and darker."

"What do you mean that you never saw the rebel leader hurting Taylor?" I asked.

"I told you that she might have been sexually assaulted right before you and Hudson left for Lania," Harlow reminded me. "I really think it's true."

"She never mentioned it to you?" I questioned.

Hudson and I had always suspected that Taylor had been assaulted by the rebel leader, but after Hudson had gotten closer to Taylor following her rescue, my older brother had never brought the subject up again.

For me, the fact that he *didn't* mention it was further proof that it happened.

Harlow shook her head. "She's never talked about it. I think I'm going to have to ask her straight out, but in my gut, I know she was sexually assaulted."

She stopped speaking, and I could tell she was focused on a group of people walking toward us.

I squeezed her hand. Any adult-sized person was a threat to her right now, but I could clearly see the college emblem on their shirts. "It's just a bunch of students, Harlow. Everything is fine."

I watched as Molly moved to form a perimeter beside and in front of Harlow by moving back and forth in the space so nobody got too close.

"I'm sorry," she said once the group had passed, sounding embarrassed. "I guess I'm still on edge."

"Don't apologize," I grumbled. "You're out here walking even though you're anxious. Give yourself credit for that. How's the knee?" I guided Harlow around a corner so we could walk in a square instead of retracing our steps back to her apartment.

"It's good. I'm not sure what Marshall told you, but it's never been horribly painful."

"It should have been completely healed by now," I grumbled.

"It's mostly my fault," she acknowledged. "It probably would be better if I'd done my home exercises after physical therapy, and if I hadn't been so isolated that I didn't walk much. I just wasn't really motivated to do anything because I was always so tired."

Yeah, that shit happened when someone was sleep-deprived, anxious, depressed, guilt-ridden, grief-stricken, and felt like they had no real purpose in life anymore.

Fuck! If I'd known just how bad things were going for Harlow, I would have nipped this shit in the bud a long time ago.

Before she'd gotten sleep-deprived because of her nightmares.

Before she'd sunk into a deep depression and anxiety.

Before she'd had a chance to completely internalize her guilt.

Before she'd suffered more than she already had from the kidnapping.

I felt like Last Hope and Montgomery Mining had completely failed her.

Hell, worse than that, I felt like *I'd* failed her, and I had no damn idea why I was feeling that way. Harlow and I weren't exactly friends, and we'd never been lovers. But for some reason, I felt connected to her in a way I couldn't explain, even if I wanted to try to find a rational reason for it.

Honestly, I was certain that unexplainable connection had been the reason I'd reached out to be her advisor in the first place. I'd needed to know she was doing okay after what she'd been through.

She's not okay, and I wish to hell I'd known that a lot earlier.

Unfortunately, after seeing her today, the previous agreement I'd made with Harlow wasn't going to cut it. A few hours a week with her wasn't going to help me accomplish what I needed to get done as soon as possible.

"I need to change up our advisor agreement a little," I said, already knowing I was going to get some pushback.

She turned her head to look at me. "Before we talk about our agreement, I need a favor," she said hesitantly.

Okay, this could work. If she needed something from me, maybe we could work out some kind of deal. "Shoot. What do you need?"

She took a deep breath. "If you haven't already, I'd appreciate it if you don't share this whole advisor situation with Hudson right now. Taylor is so happy, and if she finds out that I'm not doing well, she'll worry. She thinks I'm doing okay. I'd prefer to let her continue to assume that for a little while longer."

Fuck! Just when Harlow should be reaching out to Taylor, she'd obviously shut her down. Taylor was doing great, and I knew she'd be the first one to support Harlow if the stubborn woman had just given her a chance. "You do realize that you'll eventually have to tell her the truth so the two of you can talk."

She nodded. "Yes. I just don't want to do that right now. Please. I'd like to get my head on straight before I try to get her to tell me what really happened."

Maybe it's better this way, for now.

"I haven't said a word about this to Hudson. The only ones who know are me and Marshall. I can make sure it stays that way until you feel like you're ready to come clean with Taylor," I agreed. "I'm not saying I think it's the right thing to do because I think Taylor would be there for you if you needed her. But I respect your right to keep it private."

"Thanks," she answered, sounding relieved. "Now tell me how you want to change our agreement."

I took a deep breath.

I was a co-CEO of a company that was a global giant, but I felt like I'd never gone into making a deal as important as the one I was about to attempt right now.

Chapter 5

Harlow

"I don't think my knee is quite a hundred percent, but it doesn't hurt at all anymore," I told Jax as I swam in his ridiculously large pool. "I think it just needs to get a little stronger."

Jax had picked me up from my apartment and brought me to his gorgeous Coronado Island home every single day for the last two weeks.

Usually, he arrived around four in the afternoon, and our routine was always the same.

We worked out in his gym, my exercises gentle and modified to help get my knee stronger.

After that, we always hit the pool, usually with a glass of wine, and grabbed some dinner before he took me back home.

Our walks and talks had gotten lengthier, and my trust in Jax had grown over the last two weeks.

I saw Dr. Romero every single morning, and in addition to traditional therapy, she was also doing EMDR, which seemed to be helping me enormously. I'd been a little skeptical that anything could help reprocess any of my bad memories, much less desensitize me enough to not react to triggers. Fortunately, I'd discovered that all of my doubts had been unfounded. As Dr. Romero had hoped, those sessions had started working soon after I'd finished the second one. After that, I seemed to improve a little more every day.

My horrible nightmares had stopped, but I partly credited my new canine companion for that. I sometimes woke up startled at night, only to find that Molly was nudging me to wake up. I was completely convinced that the adorable little monster could actually sense when I was falling into a nightmare. I had no clue whether it was some kind of restlessness or noises I made when I was sleeping that tipped her off. All I knew was that it was easy to fall back to sleep since I didn't wake up screaming and traumatized.

"I'm starting to get hungry," Jax informed me from his lounger beside the pool.

His swims didn't usually last all that long. Maybe because he was used to having this amazing pool available all the time. But me? I lingered in the water as long as possible. There was something magical about being in the infinity edge pool with sweeping, panoramic views of the bay, and watching the lights across the water as the city began to light up at dusk.

I rolled my eyes. "Is there *ever* a time when you're *not* hungry?" I asked, amused. Jax could put away more food than any person I'd ever known.

"We just finished a tough workout, and then a swim. That works up my appetite," he argued.

"*You* did a tough workout," I reminded him. "I did a sissy workout that wouldn't even qualify as exercise."

Jax petted Tango, his golden retriever, as he answered, "It's exactly what you need to heal that knee up completely. You can argue all you want about the easy workouts, but you're not doing anything more than what's necessary until you're ready to push a little harder."

I'd *never* be able to push myself like Jax did, even if my knee was just like new. The man was brutal when it came to physical fitness, which probably had a lot to do with his Special Forces background, and the fact that he was involved in Last Hope.

Yeah, I was previous military, and before the kidnapping, I'd kept active enough to stay in shape, but I hadn't tortured myself like Jax did every single day.

"God, you're so bossy it's almost annoying," I retorted as I floated on my back. "You're lucky that I'm way too tired to argue with you right now."

Okay, maybe he wasn't *always* high-handed, but I'd gotten my first taste of Jax's stubborn tendencies two weeks ago, and he could be a tyrant when he really wanted something.

He'd been pretty damn pushy about me meeting with him every single day, and he'd made it clear that he wouldn't recommend that Marshall even consider the possibility of me being part of Last Hope unless I agreed. Oh, he hadn't exactly *threatened* me if I didn't meet with him every single day. Jaxton Montgomery could be extremely charming while he was getting his own way.

In the end, I'd agreed to four weeks of working with Jax every single day because I'd wanted to get better.

I'd also been aware that Jax was going to give up a lot of his valuable free time to try to help a woman he barely knew. He'd rearranged his work schedule by going in early so he could pick me up at a reasonable hour in the late afternoon. Really, how many men like Jax Montgomery were willing to rearrange their life to help one of their lower-level employees?

This entire advisor relationship is nothing like I thought it would be.

Every single day, I learned something new about Jax that touched me, and those discoveries made me realize that nearly every assumption I'd ever made about him was completely...wrong.

"I'd offer to cook, but that's not exactly one of my many talents," he said drily.

I swam over to where his chair was positioned, rested my arms on the concrete and looked up at him. "Do you mean there's one area where you *don't* excel?"

Since Jax had a genius IQ that was off the charts, and was an incredibly curious guy, sometimes he seemed like a very sexy, walking, talking encyclopedia.

"There's more than one of those areas, actually," he confessed.

"If there is, I haven't found them," I teased as I splashed water at him playfully. "But it's nice to know you have one or two flaws. A perfect man who knows everything would be incredibly boring."

He grinned. "But my dysfunction in the kitchen still leaves us with a dinner issue."

Jax had a housekeeper who came in during the week, and always left a delicious dinner for us every night. But since it was Saturday, we were on our own. We'd ordered out the weekend before, so I offered, "I'll cook. I don't mind. I'm sure you have plenty of food in that gigantic kitchen of yours."

I exited the pool and grabbed the towel on the lounger next to Jax's.

He shook his head. "You're not here to work, Harlow."

"It's not like I've been doing much work at all lately," I mumbled. "I actually do like to cook."

"Sit first, and drink the glass of wine I brought you earlier. I'm not really *that* hungry yet," he told me.

The moment I sat, and grabbed my wine from the small table between me and Jax, Molly joined me in the oversized lounge chair. She stretched out next to me, and plopped her head in my lap.

I stroked her soft fur as I said with a sigh, "I'm not sure how I'm ever going to give Molly up when you decide you have to have her back."

Technically, I wasn't even allowed to have a dog in my apartment. It wasn't that the building didn't allow them, but each unit was individually owned. My landlord did not allow pets. Period. Somehow, Jax had gotten him to change his mind. I was fairly certain bribery had been involved. Jax had changed the subject every time I'd asked how he'd managed to convince my pet-*unfriendly* landlord to agree to Molly staying at my place.

Jax petted his golden retriever's head. "Since Tango and I have visiting rights every day, I think we're handling it okay."

I took a sip of a very good white wine, and admired the breathtaking view of the city lights across the bay. "This is such an amazing house, but I guess I never took you as a Coronado Island kind of guy," I told him.

Not that the peninsula didn't have some very expensive homes, and Jax's estate was one of those pricey properties. Maybe I'd seen him as more of a downtown San Diego, luxury penthouse type of person. Coronado had more of a smaller town, historic vibe, even though it could be crowded and packed with tourists during the busy season.

He turned his head and looked at me, pinning me with his gorgeous, emerald-eyed gaze. "Why not? There's plenty of SEALs wandering around to make me feel at home, and I've always liked it here. There's even an off-leash dog beach here. Not many of those around anymore."

I shook my head. "I didn't even know they had one. Even though I'm a California native, I haven't spent much time here. I guess I was assuming you were more of a downtown kind of guy who would want to be closer to your headquarters."

He shrugged. "I have a condo within walking distance of the offices. I used it a lot when I first got out of the Navy, and had to put in a lot of long hours, but I seldom stay there anymore since I got this place. The dogs are good by themselves during the day since they have the electronic dog door, and the place is completely fenced. Plus, my housekeeper is here a lot, and she loves the mutts. But I don't really want to leave them alone all night."

My heart melted. How many filthy rich men like Jax were willing to put their dogs' needs before their own?

Yeah, he liked his expensive cars, nice homes, and custom suits for the office, but there was so much more to this man than just what people saw on the surface.

"It's so peaceful and quiet here," I said as I laid back against the headrest of the lounger.

"Which is one of the reasons I like living here," he shared. "I wanted my privacy, and most of the nosy reporters don't follow me around here. Since I've never brought any of my dates here, I guess they don't feel it's worth their time to hunt me down outside of the city."

"You've never brought any of your dates here?" I asked curiously.

"Never," Jax confirmed. "Let's face it, there's a lot more to do off the island. It's pretty quiet here compared to downtown San Diego."

I was dying to ask him how he got laid if he'd never brought a woman here. Did he use his downtown condo? Or did they always go to her place?

Jax's sex life is none of my business. I am not going to ask that question, no matter how curious I might be.

"Then I'm really honored that you trust me enough to bring *me* here. Not that we're dating, or that I think any of these visits are anything like a date," I hurried to assure him. "I mean, we've mostly just learned to tolerate each other, right?"

Oh hell, that hadn't come out quite right.

And it wasn't really the truth, either.

"I'm sorry," I rushed to add. "It's more than that. As strange as it might seem, I actually like you, and I'd like to think we're becoming friends. I just didn't want you to think I was hitting on you or anything."

Jax chuckled. "Believe me, that's the last thing I'd assume since you laughed in my face when I asked you to go out with me. I'm not just tolerating you, either, Harlow. I like spending time with you. Our relationship isn't just about my obligation to you as an advisor anymore. It's nice hanging out with a woman who doesn't have a shitload of preconceived ideas about who I should be because of my wealth and my last name."

I squirmed in my chair just a little, maybe because I'd been guilty of prejudging Jax in the past. "I'm sorry I laughed at you two years ago when you asked me out," I told him earnestly. "I could have been a lot nicer about it."

After spending more time with Jax, I'd realized that regardless of his reputation and his preferences for one-off dating experiences, he was a pretty nice guy.

"I can't really say that I blame you," Jax answered contemplatively. "My dates usually do turn into a media circus. Some women thrive on that kind of attention, but I can see that you aren't the type to enjoy having reporters in your face."

"It wasn't all about that," I told him truthfully. "I'm almost thirty-two years old, and I was thirty when you asked me out. I was beyond my party years, and ready to look for a relationship that meant something. I guess I was looking for more than casual dates or a dance partner at a club. I was kind of done with those relationships."

"And you assumed I was just another player?" he asked, sounding slightly wounded.

Our gazes locked, and my heart skipped a beat. A woman could so easily get lost in his mercurial green eyes. "Of course I did," I said softly. "How could I not? You're the insanely handsome, highly desirable billionaire who has never gone on a second date with a woman."

He held my gaze as he replied, "What if I'd just never found a woman who was more interested in me than my money and my last name?"

I swallowed hard. "Then I'd say that they were missing out."

Was that *really* why he'd never asked a woman out twice? Surely some of those women had seen something more than Jax's money and status.

He was so much more than just those two things.

He shook his head and turned away. "It doesn't really matter, I guess. You *did* turn me down, and now I'm your advisor and a friend. I can't say that I'm completely unhappy about how everything worked out, even if you did break my heart at the time."

I snorted because I knew he was being dramatic to make me smile. "I think the only thing that I wounded was your ego, and I think you already have far too many women who fall all over you. Everybody needs a reality check once in a while."

"Maybe," he said noncommittally. "So, did you find that *something more* relationship you wanted with Mark?"

I was silent for a moment, thinking about his question before I answered. "In a way, yes. He was one of the kindest men I'd ever known, and we became close enough that I was comfortable sharing almost everything with him. We were definitely friends who flirted with the idea of a romance, but we never really had enough time to figure out all the other stuff. We didn't go on real dates that often because he was always in another country on another job. Maybe it could have been more, so I think I'm grieving the loss of what could have been had we just gotten more time. Not to mention losing the first man I'd really cared for and trusted in a very long time."

"Obviously, you've had other boyfriends, right?" Jax questioned.

Because that was a topic I didn't want to delve into very deeply, I replied in a lighthearted tone. "I doubt very many women get to my age without having kissed a whole lot of frogs."

"No princes?" he teased.

I sighed. "Sadly, not a single one turned into two-legged royalty after I kissed them. I guess the closest I'll get to knowing a prince is my conversations with Nick."

Jax raised an eyebrow. "Nick? As in Crown Prince Niklaos of Lania? *That* Nick? You actually talk to that bastard?"

I was taken aback because Jax had suddenly gotten so serious.

I nodded. "Occasionally. We do video chats from time to time. He keeps in touch just to see how I'm doing. He actually owns a home in Newport Beach. We've spoken a few times about getting together when he comes for a visit."

"Not happening. Ever," he growled.

I turned my head sharply to look at his face to see if he was joking. One look at his stony, stubborn expression gave me my answer.

Chapter 6

Jax

"Have you forgotten that Prince Niklaos is the ruler of the country where you were nearly killed?" I asked in a guttural voice.

Christ! Just the thought of Harlow cozying up to Prince Nick made my blood boil.

Yeah, I'd only met the guy in person once, but I hadn't trusted him then, and I didn't trust him now.

Maybe my older brother Hudson was convinced that Nick had no part in the kidnapping of three of our employees, but I wasn't. Since two of them had almost died, and the other one had been executed mercilessly, it was going to take more than just the prince's word that he hadn't been involved to change my mind.

Hell, even if he hadn't participated in the event, the asshole was at least *partially* responsible since it was his damn country. Those rebels hadn't just showed up in Lania right before the incident. They'd been hiding out in that country for some time before it occurred.

"It wasn't really his fault, even though he feels responsible," Harlow said. "The rebels were in a remote area, and it's a really large island nation. The majority of the population is along the coastline and in and near the capital."

"Not his fault?" I said irritably. "How can it not be his fault? Where in the hell was his domestic intel? He should have had some clue that there were still terrorist groups present. I lost at least a half dozen friends to that damn country and their rebels when I was a SEAL. They haven't been a peaceful country long enough for them to have let their guard down."

"Jax, their military isn't sophisticated enough to function like ours, and their government doesn't have an equal to our FBI and other governmental law enforcement. Give the poor guy a break. He hasn't been the ruler of Lania for long, and it will take some time for him to turn things around there. Like you said, they were a country in a brutal civil war for a long time."

"I can't believe you're defending him after all you went through," I grumbled unhappily.

Harlow shrugged. "If I'm going to believe that all this was just a fluke incident, I can hardly blame Nick. I've spoken to him enough to know that he really does want to change things in Lania. He grew up and went to college in England, and he truly believes that Lania should be a democracy. He'd love to see things change until the royal family of Lania functions much like it does in England. Unfortunately, that isn't going to happen overnight since Lania has been ruled by the royal family for centuries."

Jesus Christ! Harlow had obviously been totally brainwashed by that royal prick.

I ground my teeth, trying to stay calm. "How do you know that everything he's telling you isn't all a lie? What if he wanted to stir up trouble so he could look like a hero when all of the guerillas were captured? He's a new ruler, and his ideas to modernize Lania haven't been all that popular with the people. Now, the country idolizes him because they think he's a damn genius for simply arresting and imprisoning the rebels after *we* found them, *and* pulled our final living hostage out ourselves."

Harlow shot me an annoyed look. "Nick would never do something like that just to get the approval of the population."

"Dictators do horrific things all the time for just that reason," I reminded her. "We both know that."

She sighed. "I suppose. But I trust Nick. We video chat, and I've never seen a single sign that he's being deceptive. He has such warm and sympathetic eyes. Maybe that sounds naïve, but it's my gut instinct."

Hell, I couldn't really argue that gut instinct meant nothing. Mine had saved my ass enough times out in the field that I couldn't discount it. "Just be careful," I warned her. "Murderers can be extremely charming until they pull out a gun and start shooting."

"I understand that," she agreed, sounding frustrated. "But I'm not turning my back on Nick. He's been extremely supportive since the whole thing happened, and I don't think it's an act. At times, he's been the *only* person I could talk to because I can't really share much of this with my friends. Or my mother, either, for that matter. I'm too afraid I'll accidentally expose Last Hope."

At that moment, I pretty much hated myself for not being there when Harlow had needed to talk.

Yeah, I could be a dick sometimes, but I would have been a better confidant than...Prince Nick.

More than likely, all Nick really wanted was to seduce Harlow when he visited the US.

Hell, what red-blooded male *wouldn't* want that?

Even though I knew she was vulnerable, I sure as hell couldn't make myself stop thinking about getting Harlow naked. And fuck knew I'd tried. Hard.

The majority of the time, I'd kept my mind out of the gutter because her mental and physical wellbeing meant more to me than a fuck. Nevertheless, my brain *did* go there sometimes. I wasn't a damn saint, and I couldn't always control how my dick reacted whenever she was around. I just chose to ignore that reaction... most of the time.

Shit! Maybe I *was* overreacting to the fact that Harlow chose to have a relationship with the ruler of the country that had nearly killed her. It wasn't my right to tell her who she could and couldn't decide to call a friend.

I just fucking hated the idea of her getting too close to *that* bastard.

Prince Niklaos was way too nauseatingly charming, educated, young, and while I hated to admit it, the guy would probably be considered attractive by most women.

I ignored the small hint of possessiveness that had been eating at me since Harlow had mentioned that she was in contact with Prince Nick. It was natural for me to be protective, right? I was her advisor, her employer, and her...friend.

"What about Marshall?" I asked. "He's been in touch since the beginning."

Harlow swallowed a sip of her wine before she replied, "I adore Marshall, and he's been one of the few constants in my life since this happened. But he acts like my father most of the time. And I think that you've worked with him long enough to know he isn't exactly warm and fuzzy. There are lines he doesn't cross, and things he doesn't talk about."

"Yeah, I get it," I agreed. "I think he was a SEAL team leader for too long. He throws out a command, and expects everyone to fall in line without question. He's a damn good man, and one I'm always glad is covering my ass, but he's not an easy person to have a personal conversation with most of the time."

"But his heart is always in the right place," Harlow mused.

"Agreed," I told her. "But you have me now. You know you can talk to me about anything, right?"

If Harlow was going to spill her guts, I'd prefer she did it with me instead of Prince Nick.

She nodded slowly as a ghost of a smile formed on her lips. "*Almost* anything. It's not like we're lifelong friends, and a woman has to have some secrets."

Fuck that! I was going to get Harlow to trust me enough to tell me *anything*. I had no damn idea why that was really necessary, but it *was* going to happen.

Doing my duty as her advisor, and then going our separate ways just wasn't going to cut it for me anymore.

I was getting addicted to Harlow's presence, and I was going to make damn sure this friendship didn't end after the four weeks we'd agreed upon.

In my mind, because we hadn't made a deal on anything *after* that four weeks, it was open for negotiation.

Honestly, I hoped that after four weeks, she'd hang out with me because she wanted to, not because she *had* to do it as part of some agreement.

Harlow yawned before she said, "I guess I should have skipped the wine tonight."

I scrutinized her face as I asked, "Did you sleep okay last night?"

She shot me a genuine smile, and my dick was instantly hard.

Harlow was slowly improving, and I didn't take a single one of those smiles for granted since it had rarely happened in the beginning.

"I told you that I'm sleeping just fine," she assured me. "I think the wine just made me a little tired because I ate an early lunch. I probably just need to go make something for dinner."

"If you're hungry, I can just order out," I told her.

"Absolutely not," she insisted. "I'm making dinner, and I doubt I'll fade away from hunger before it's done."

"I should have ordered earlier," I grumbled. "I'd prefer that you never have to go hungry again."

Harlow had curves in all the right places, but she didn't carry any extra weight, so the food deprivation she'd suffered during her imprisonment had definitely shown. She'd been too thin when she'd first gotten released as a hostage.

"I'll eventually make up for those lost meals. Wilma is an amazing cook," she said, referring to my housekeeper's culinary skills in an amused tone. "Taylor and I used to dream about all the things we'd eat once we got released. It's weird what you'll do when you're in captivity to avoid going crazy."

"What did you think about?" I asked.

She laughed. "Good Mexican and Thai food, and ice cream."

"And have you gotten your fill of all of those things now?"

"I wish," she replied wistfully. "I got my groceries delivered once I got back to my apartment, and Ben & Jerry's was always on the shopping list. Unfortunately, most of the good Thai and Mexican restaurants aren't in my area. Hopefully, now that I'm doing better, I'll get to all of my favorites, eventually."

My gut ached when I thought about how isolated Harlow must have felt over the last several months. She'd lost Mark, and it was evident that he was the person she'd talked to the most. She'd been intentionally distant with Taylor because of her perceived guilt about putting her friend in a bad situation. Then, because she'd had no real outlet or help dealing with the trauma of her experience, the depression and anxiety had set in. She'd eventually become a victim of her own fear and guilt, which had gotten so bad that she'd confined herself in her small apartment alone.

Nobody knew better than I did just how dangerous it was to be way too alone with just your own thoughts. If a person already felt like they were on the edge, that shit could push them right over the cliff.

Luckily, I'd had family available, and Hudson and Cooper could relate because we'd all had similar experiences.

Harlow had no siblings, and she hadn't felt comfortable spilling her guts to her mother. She'd been utterly and completely alone with her own thoughts, without a single coping mechanism.

Christ! It was a miracle she was still sane.

"Why don't you stay here tonight?" I suggested impulsively. "Tomorrow is Sunday, and we'd have the whole day to knock around town if you feel up to it. There's a great Mexican restaurant there, and some of the best ice cream in the entire San Diego area."

Harlow had stashed some extra clothing, a second bathing suit, and workout clothing in the coat closet. She always took a shower after she left the pool, and put on clean clothing, so she couldn't refuse because she didn't have a change of clothes.

Truth was, I really wanted to spend the day with Harlow, but I wasn't going to push her if she didn't feel ready to sit down in a restaurant. Sometimes we took a walk after dinner, but my neighborhood was as quiet as a graveyard after dark.

Harlow chewed on her lip for a moment before she said, "It's always busy in the downtown area."

"It can be," I agreed. I didn't bullshit Harlow, and I didn't plan on starting to do it now. "But we are starting the off-season for tourists, so it's not as bad as it is in the summer."

Her expression was still pensive as she said, "God, I really want to do it, but I haven't really been out in crowds yet."

"I have an extra bicycle. We could bike our way around to most places. I think your knee will hold up fine if we take it slow." It was pathetic how badly I wanted her to give it a try.

Harlow was ready to take these steps, and it would be a much smoother road if she didn't do it alone. To be honest, I didn't want her to attempt a milestone like this by herself. If she faltered, I wanted to be there to give her the support she needed.

"You mean I'd be spared from riding in one of your rocket ship vehicles," she joked weakly, still sounding somewhat apprehensive.

"You know you're actually starting to enjoy riding in my cars," I answered. "You're getting addicted to feeling the power of zero to sixty in under three seconds."

"Maybe it's not so bad," she admitted. "But I still think they're completely inefficient."

I chuckled, knowing that was the strongest capitulation I was going to get right now. "So what do you say? Are you ready to be a bum with me tomorrow? You know if you're not comfortable, we can nix the whole thing and come back here, right?"

"I don't want to ruin your whole day off if that happens," she said uncertainly.

"You won't. There's nobody I'd rather hang out with, no matter what we're doing, so you might as well say yes." Okay, I was pushing, but I knew she wanted this, and she definitely needed it.

She nodded slowly and got to her feet. "Okay, I'll give it my best shot. I think I'll be fine as long as you're with me. It would be amazing to be able to get outside for the whole day, and the island is beautiful. Thank you for offering to spend the day with me."

I knew that her agreement to venture downtown and around the island was a silent statement about how much she trusted *me*.

As I got my ass out of my chair to go see what I could do to help with dinner, I swore I'd do whatever it took to make sure Harlow always knew she'd be safe with me.

Chapter 7

Harlow

"Hey, Harlow, are you still okay?" Jax asked as his concerned eyes roamed over my face.

He reached across the table in the Mexican restaurant, took my hand in his, and gently squeezed.

I automatically stroked my thumb over the back of his hand as I said, "I'm good. I guess I zoned out for a minute. I was doing one of Dr. Romero's mini meditation techniques."

God, I was getting addicted to the way this man never hesitated to reach out to me whenever he thought I might be panicked.

Sometimes, it felt like Jax and I were constantly connected in some weird way that I didn't even completely understand.

Not that I'd totally figured out the complicated and occasionally infuriating man, but I was starting to pick up on some of his subtle body language. More than likely, he was doing the same with me.

"Are you nervous?" he asked pensively. "The minute you start feeling uncomfortable, we're out of here."

I sent him a don't-you-dare-get-out-of-that-chair look. "Are you kidding? I just ordered fresh swordfish tacos, a lobster quesadilla, and a gigantic strawberry margarita. You'd have to drag me out of here to get me to leave before I devour that food."

I couldn't say that I hadn't had a few brief hesitations during the day, but I'd never been truly afraid. The town was busy, especially near the famous Hotel del Coronado, but it wasn't as crazy crowded as it was in the summer months or during the holidays.

"I'm never going to be the guy who drags you away from your food," Jax teased. "I was just checking in."

Yeah, Jax did that a lot. *Checking in.* Not that I was complaining. The gesture was far more comforting than it was annoying. Maybe that was why I'd been able to enjoy myself so much today. The guy worried enough for both of us.

"I had fun today," I assured him. "It's the best day I've had in a long time."

"I'm not so sure doing the entire bike path around the island was such a great idea," Jax rumbled. "How's the knee holding up? It was a long ride."

I smiled. "It was good for my soul, and my knee is fine. I told you that it doesn't hurt at all anymore."

Lord knew that Jax had gone overboard protecting my knee this morning. He had applied a compression bandage before we'd left his place for added support. And he'd babied the crap out of me by stopping every ten minutes on the bike trail for a break.

"I get that," he replied gruffly. "But you're supposed to go slow with the exercise."

"I'm not out of shape," I informed him. "I just had a minor knee injury."

He shook his head as he put his empty water glass on the table. "It wasn't minor. You had a grade 2 tear to your MCL, Harlow."

"And it's healed now," I said gently. "I just need to strengthen the whole knee so it doesn't happen again. Honestly, that ride made me feel like I was more at peace with myself than I've been for a long time. I think I forgot how much fun it is to just get on a bike and cruise. If I ever meet your sister, Riley, I'll definitely be thanking her for the temporary use of her bike. That's one very sweet beach cruiser."

The bicycle was a really pretty teal color trimmed in black, but the way it handled was what made it really stand out. It was nimble, lightweight, and quick. Obviously, Riley liked to be comfortable, too. My ass had never been so well padded while I was riding a bike.

"She hasn't ridden it in a long time," Jax mused. "She used to come out to the island more often, but now that she's married, we usually all get together at her place in Citrus Beach. Riley is much better at organizing family gatherings, and her beach property there is huge."

I nodded. "She's been so good to Taylor, and I'm grateful for that. I think every time Taylor starts to feel a little lost in the world of the ultra-wealthy, Riley has been there to help her," I said wistfully. "I think I'd like your sister. It sounds like she's really down-to-earth."

"I love my sister dearly, but she can be a redheaded menace when she wants to be," Jax grumbled. "But I've never met a woman with a kinder heart, and yeah, she's very…normal. None of us hang out with the elite crowd if we can help it."

"Do you get along well with her husband?" I asked curiously.

He raised a brow. "Seth? Yeah, he's one of us now. We've gotten along just fine ever since the day he completely understood that if he hurt our sister, my brothers and I would cut his balls off."

I snorted. "Oh, my God. That poor man. I can only imagine how intimidating it was for him to have to pass the big-brother test *three times.*"

"It wasn't all that hard," Jax said. "Seth is a good man. He's worked his ass off to build a successful real estate corporation from the ground up. He came from pretty humble beginnings, and most of his adult life was dedicated to helping his older brother raise their younger siblings. Plus, it's almost nauseatingly obvious that he worships the ground Riley walks on. All any of us have ever wanted was for her to be happy."

Jax released my hand as the waiter arrived with our drinks. I smiled as the server plopped down a big strawberry margarita in front of me before he walked away.

Jax had ordered the same, minus the strawberry.

Once our waiter had departed, Jax asked jokingly, "Am I going to have to worry about whether you'll be capable of drinking and biking?"

I raised a brow in challenge. "I was a technical sergeant in the United States Air Force. We airmen know how to handle our liquor, sailor. I could drink a lot of my fellow airmen under the table," I teased. "I think I can still ride straight after one watered-down margarita."

I wasn't much of a drinker anymore, but I'd certainly done my share of nights out, and drinking challenges in the military when I was younger. Most of my companions had been male since the total Air Force personnel was eighty percent men.

Really, any female member of the military had no choice but to get used to being surrounded by large amounts of testosterone every day.

Jax smirked as he lifted his glass. "Cheers."

I smacked my glass with his before I took a sip, and instantly realized the drink wasn't the least bit watered down. "I guess they're more generous than most places with the tequila," I said to Jax as I put my glass back down on the table.

"Did you really think I'd take you to a Mexican place with lousy food and watered-down margaritas?" he asked drily.

The restaurant was very clean, with colorful décor, but it wasn't what I'd consider an upscale place. It was exactly the kind of Mexican restaurant that generally had the best, authentic food. Apparently, Jax preferred good food over ambience.

"Probably not," I confessed as I stirred the margarita with the over-sized straw. "You apparently have very good taste in restaurants."

Jax and I had talked about our favorite places to eat in San Diego. Some of his were my favorites, too, but a few were so pricey that I'd never been able to convince myself to try them.

"There's a few of them you still need to try," he reminded me.

"The outrageously expensive ones are out," I said firmly. "I don't mind paying the price for good food, but a few of your favorites are ridiculously overpriced."

"Do we not pay you enough as a research geoscientist to try them out?" he asked. "Or for you to get a nicer apartment? I know it's not like you live in a bad area, but that place is tiny, and everything is really outdated."

"I'm just one person," I said defensively. "Why do I need a bigger place? And you pay me plenty. I just choose to use that generous salary to save. I'd like to buy my own place someday." I took a deep breath and released it slowly before I asked, "You don't have any idea what it's like to have to save for anything, do you?"

I didn't mean for the question to be an insult. It was just…fact. Jax had been outrageously wealthy since the day he was born.

"I don't," he said reluctantly. "If I want a new home, I buy it. Hell, if I want *anything*, I buy it. It wasn't my intention to offend you, Harlow. I was just thinking that maybe we needed to reevaluate our pay scale for geoscientists with a doctorate degree."

Jax looked so contrite that I felt bad I'd asked that question in the first place. "You don't. Montgomery pays more than any other company in the country would for my job title and education. There's also plenty of opportunity for advancement. I could have a nicer apartment, and I could probably put out some cash for a fancy restaurant, but I'm looking at the more tangible reward. Real estate prices are outrageous here, and I do want to be a homeowner. I shouldn't have asked you that question, Jax. It was rude, and it's not your fault that you were born filthy rich and have never had to worry about money. I guess I just can't even fathom what that kind of life would be like."

Our waiter arrived with our food before Jax could say anything else.

He devoured two of his tacos, and washed them down with his margarita before he finally replied, "Just because a person is born wealthy doesn't mean they're automatically happy. My siblings and I may have won the financial lottery, but we got completely screwed in other areas to make up for it."

I paused with a forkful of quesadilla as I asked, "What do you mean?"

"We had money, but not a very happy childhood," he grumbled. "There were plenty of times when I was a kid that I would have traded all the material things for parents who weren't total monsters."

"Explain," I requested softly.

He shook his head. "Not happening. Not right now. I'd rather enjoy my dinner. So let's talk about you instead. I get that you're saving to buy a home, but when was the last time you did or bought something frivolous just because you wanted it? You have to have some short-term rewards occasionally, Harlow."

Jax had very smoothly sidestepped my questions about his childhood. Now I was so curious to find out what he'd meant that I wanted to push for more, but I didn't. He'd respected my boundaries, and I wanted to do the same for him. Hopefully, he'd talk more about himself someday. I understood that he was my advisor, but I was tired of all conversations revolving around me and my issues.

I pushed the empty plate aside once I'd savored the last bite of my lobster quesadilla, and put my swordfish tacos in front of me.

"I do some stuff occasionally," I said, being intentionally evasive.

He caught my gaze and lifted a brow. "And what would that *stuff* be, exactly?"

Okay. Yeah. So he'd seen right through that answer. "I did a full spa day with a friend."

"When?" he pushed.

"A year and a half ago," I mumbled, refusing to tell him that the spa had been running an amazing special on full spa days that week.

"Right. So it's been a while. What else? Tell me something from the last year," he insisted.

I let out an exasperated breath. "I'm not a high-maintenance kind of woman. I worked long hours in the lab fairly often, and that's what I really wanted to do. When I'm rolling on a project, I can't just shut that down and go home. Once I did get back to my apartment, I was perfectly happy going for a run, and grabbing an easy dinner at home. If I had time, I'd watch one of the TV shows that I record, or talk to Mark if the time difference worked for whatever part of the world he was in at the time. It didn't take much to make me happy.

Okay, so maybe I'm one of the most boring single women on the planet, but I'm just not into the party or club scene."

He studied me for a moment before he replied calmly, "Believe me, women who troll the clubs every night are far from exciting. They're obsessed with appearances at the beginning of the evening, only to end up vomiting on their expensive high-heeled shoes by the end of the night. Have you ever tried to have a decent conversation with a woman whose biggest tragedy is breaking a freshly manicured fingernail? No? Well, I have, and it's pure torture. I'd take what you consider boring over *that* any day of the week."

The pained look on his face made me laugh so hard I nearly choked on my taco.

The thought of Jax trying to have a conversation with a drunken club hopper who had just broken a fingernail made me laugh a little harder.

"Somehow, I just can't see you hanging out with that crowd," I said once I'd caught my breath.

"I have," he assured me. "But that phase didn't last very long."

I could definitely understand why that scene had gotten old for him in a hurry. "I've done it myself, and I decided I'd much rather be home reading a book or watching TV when I had free time. Until a few years ago, I was always working full-time and going to school. So I'd much rather spend my free time doing something more relaxing now that I actually have a little time to myself."

"You're an intelligent, beautiful woman, Harlow. You never made time to date before Mark?" he asked huskily.

"I never had much time," I explained. "I got up, went to work, and then to classes. I'd fall into bed every night because I was exhausted. The next day it was pretty much rinse and repeat until I got my doctorate."

"Until you met Mark?" he questioned.

I sighed. Jax was tenacious when he wanted to know something. "I was engaged once, a long time ago. It didn't work out, and it took me a long time to get over it. I dated before I met Mark, but none of those relationships exactly turned into anything meaningful."

"Do you want to tell me about your engagement?"

"No," I said simply. "I'd rather not talk about it."

That had been a painful time in my life, and I'd much rather *not* open that door again.

"Then we won't talk about it right now," he agreed. "I think you have enough on your plate at the moment, but I think you'll tell me someday."

"Maybe when *you* decide to tell me about your parents and your childhood," I shot back, keeping my tone light.

He looked disgruntled as he muttered, "In that case, it could be a while before I hear about it."

We switched to lighter topics while we finished off our margaritas.

After doing daily, very intense therapy sessions, it was a relief not to discuss heavier subjects.

Jax had a gift for telling amusing stories, and he kept me laughing until we exited the building.

"It's good to hear you laugh, Harlow," Jax said in a husky voice as he took my hand for the short walk to our bikes.

I sighed. "It's good to be able to laugh," I confessed. "Thank you for such an amazing day."

"Let's not end it yet," he suggested. "We can go pick up the dogs and take them to the dog beach for a while."

It wasn't like I had anything to do in my empty apartment, but… "You have to be tired of looking at me by now, Jax. It's getting late."

He shot me a dubious glance. "It's not even dark yet, Harlow. And I plan on taking the dogs to the dog beach whether you agree to go or not. I'd prefer to have some human company. If you don't come, you'll miss the trip for ice cream afterward. The mutts would never forgive me if I passed the shop without getting them a doggie-size cone."

I laughed. "Okay, I'm sold."

He grinned. "Was it the beach that convinced you, or the ice cream?"

I bumped his shoulder playfully as we reached our bikes. "Did it ever occur to you that maybe I just want to spend more time with you?"

"Honestly, it didn't," he answered in a fake solemn voice. "My bet is that it was the ice cream."

Oh, Jax would lose that particular wager.

The man had no idea just how tempting it had been to spend time with him and the dogs instead of going home to a lonely apartment.

No single woman in her right mind could resist the enticing lure of being with a guy like Jax Montgomery, right?

"Think whatever you like," I quipped as I got my bike moving and headed toward Jax's place.

We were halfway to his house before I remembered that one single woman *had* resisted Jax Montgomery's charm, *and* his offer to spend time in his company.

Two years ago.

When I hadn't really known Jax.

Ironically, once upon a time, that woman had been me.

Chapter 8

Jax

I looked up as I heard the door to my office open, and saw my younger brother Cooper come in. His arms were loaded with white bags that I assumed were probably our lunch.

"Need help?" I asked.

"Nah, I got it," he answered as he kicked the door closed. "Although it would really help if you didn't order half the damn menu."

I grinned. I'd gotten used to Cooper's constantly irritable attitude during the last year or so.

When we were younger, he'd been the nicest, most good-natured Montgomery.

Now, I swore he was the surliest bastard on the planet sometimes.

Cooper hadn't been the same since he'd broken up with his last girlfriend nearly a year ago. Hudson and I knew exactly why our younger brother had become so damn cynical. We'd just never figured out who had dumped who because Cooper refused to discuss it. Hell, he wouldn't even admit that he'd been hurt.

Hudson and I had waited him out, knowing Cooper would tell us about it when he was ready.

Or so we'd thought…

"I've got an appetite, man," I complained as I snatched the bags he plopped onto the desk. "I skipped breakfast."

"Maybe because you're taking your advisor duties with Harlow way too seriously," Cooper guessed as he planted his ass in a chair on the other side of my desk. "You've been getting into the office by seven a.m. every damn morning for almost three weeks now, Jax, just so you can leave early. Have you forgotten that we own this company, and that you can come in whenever you want, and leave whenever you want?"

I'd gotten Cooper's word that he wouldn't tell Hudson about me being Harlow's advisor since she'd asked me not to tell my older brother. But Cooper and I had always been close, and I'd wanted someone other than Marshall to confide in. "I don't want to be a slacker," I told him. "I have responsibilities to take care of here, but Harlow needs somebody with her every day right now, too. It's not a big deal. I'm getting used to coming in early. I get more done when there's nobody around in the morning."

I dug into the food that Cooper had gotten from one of our favorite burger places.

"Right," Cooper said doubtfully as he unwrapped a double cheeseburger. "You do realize that you could just take a vacay, right? Hudson took time off to be with Taylor, and I spent some extra time in Seattle after our cousin Mason's wedding. When's the last time you did that yourself? If I remember right, you haven't had any real downtime in a couple of years."

"Haven't needed it," I said after taking a big slug of water to wash down my second burger.

Cooper sent me a harsh glare. "You need it," he countered. "Spending that much time with a victim is pretty intense, especially one who went through as much as she did."

I shook my head. "Weirdly, it's really not. Dr. Romero made progress with Harlow really fast because she was responsive to EMDR, and they do long cognitive sessions every day. Yeah, she's faced a lot of challenges, and she still has some ahead of her, but Harlow is a strong woman. She doesn't drag me down. In fact, it's just the opposite. I like being with her."

"Oh, fuck no," Cooper groaned. "Please don't tell me that you're getting personally involved with a woman you're supposed to be advising. You know better than that, dude."

"I'm not," I lied.

"Bullshit," Cooper answered morosely. "You're attracted to her, right? I recognize that look in your eyes. It reminds me of Hudson when he's waxing poetic about Taylor."

I probably should have known better than to stretch the truth with Cooper. He might be cranky, but he still had the best intuitive skills I'd ever seen. "Okay. So, I'm attracted to her. Hell, I have been for a long time. I met her in the lab two years ago, and I liked her so much I asked her out for dinner. She turned me down, and that was the end of it. I can't just turn off being attracted to her. But that doesn't mean I can't be her advisor and a friend."

"In what universe does that kind of arrangement work out?" Cooper scoffed. "It's completely impossible to want to fuck a woman and be her friend at the same time. The only thing that kind of arrangement will get you is blue balls, and a whole lot of heartache, Jax. I don't understand why you signed up for this in the first place."

I slammed my fist on the desk. "Because I couldn't *not* fucking do it," I growled. "I tried to get in contact with Harlow for months to talk to her about her resignation, and to convince her to take a monetary payment from Montgomery like we gave to Mark's family. Just like Taylor, she wanted nothing to do with the money. All I got was her voicemail, and an occasional hang-up. Maybe that should have been a noticeable clue that something was wrong since she'd have no problem telling me off instead of avoiding me. Unfortunately, the truth didn't knock me in the head until I started to track her progress, and I saw that she'd completely refused an advisor, or any of the other things we'd suggested. She was doing some kind of video counseling sessions with someone who had absolutely no experience treating severe emotional trauma like Harlow's. And they were only meeting once a week. Sometimes less because her so-called therapist cancelled on Harlow fairly often. *That's* why I signed up to be her advisor. I knew *something* wasn't right, and that someone had to get through to Harlow. Once I saw her in person and realized just how bad things had gotten for her, I wanted to kick myself in the ass for waiting so long."

I leaned back in my chair, knowing I'd just lost it. I was still breathing hard from releasing the pent-up frustration that had been eating at me for a long time.

Cooper released a long breath. "And you thought you were the only one who could help her?"

"I *knew* I was the only one who could get through to her. I'm probably the only person who's more stubborn than she is, and who would refuse to take *no* for an answer. Even Marshall tried to get her into decent treatment for months, and he failed," I told Cooper irritably. "Failure was not an option for me. Not after it was perfectly clear that she wasn't recovering."

"You did help her, Jax. She's on her way to recovery. She's under Dr. Romero's care. It's time for you to bail out now before you care too damn much to do that. Before it's too late."

"I do care, dammit! And it may already be too late. We've been together every single day for nearly three weeks, Coop," I explained. "Maybe you don't believe it's possible, but we have become friends. In some ways, being with Harlow has been good for me, too. You have no idea how good it feels to just be able to hang out with a woman who doesn't give a damn about my family name or my money. There's never been a female in my life like her. She actually wants to know *me*, and not the billionaire co-CEO of Montgomery. She looks at me just like she'd see any other guy, and before her, I had no idea how damn addictive that could be."

"Now I know you're completely screwed," Cooper said flatly. "What in the hell are you planning to do when she recovers, and you want more? Believe me, you *will* want more. She's already turned you down for a date, so the romantic interest obviously isn't there for her. Look, I've never met Harlow, but I honestly wish there was a chance for you two to eventually get together. She sounds like a female who would never put up with your bullshit, but obviously has the capacity to care about you and not just your money. But that ship has sailed, Jax. I never thought I'd say this since you're the king of one-nighters, but I'm afraid that you could really end up demolished when this is all over."

I shrugged. "I'm willing to take that chance. I can't just walk away."

"I was afraid you'd say that," Cooper grumbled. "Since I know I'm not going to convince you to run while you still can, just be careful."

I grinned at him. "I couldn't go very far anyway since she has custody of my dog right now, and Harlow may end up volunteering for Last Hope."

"Molly?" Cooper questioned.

I nodded and explained how Molly's training had helped Harlow.

Cooper helped out at the canine training center whenever he could, and donated heavily to the organization, too.

"It's always been a win-win situation," Cooper mused after I'd finished talking. "Shelter dogs get a good home, and veterans benefit by getting some help with their PTSD. I'm glad that Molly could help Harlow. Now, explain to me exactly how Harlow could possibly end up being a Last Hope volunteer. Has Marshall completely lost his mind?"

I went through Harlow's idea, and Marshall's rationale for considering it.

Cooper was quiet after I'd finished talking, so I finished the last of my food as I watched his contemplative expression.

I could tell that my younger brother was thinking, weighing all the pros and cons, and running through every possible scenario that could occur from making a change to Last Hope.

It was almost scary that Cooper's mind was like one big super-computer sometimes, and even more frightening because once he came to a conclusion, he was never wrong.

"It could work, as long as Marshall sticks to only tapping volunteers who already know about Last Hope," Cooper said cautiously. "We've been getting a lot more technically sophisticated for a while now, and we can hardly expect Marshall to keep learning all those areas himself. I hate to admit it, but we could really use Harlow's skills as a weather specialist volunteer. Think about how precise our data could be. It's a risk because once someone becomes an official volunteer, they'll get a lot more information about the entire operation. However, we take that risk with every previous Special Forces guy we take on, too. Granted, most of them understand how vital it is to keep our operations a secret, but it's still a bit of a crapshoot. When you're dealing with that many personalities, you'll eventually find an asshole in any group."

"Harlow still wants to volunteer just as much as she did in the very beginning," I told Cooper.

"Since she's previous military, she's obviously aware of how important it is not to out Last Hope," Cooper replied. "You do realize that if things go south with you and Harlow, it could be awkward if she's a member of Last Hope."

"That's not going to happen," I said firmly.

For now, I was going to support Harlow, and just be a friend, even if it killed me.

At some point in the future, once she'd gotten her life back, I *was* going to ask her out again, and hope to hell her answer was different the second time around.

Chapter 9

Harlow

"**N**o! Please! Stop hurting him! Mark! Noooooo!"
I woke up screaming, and my body shot up into a
sitting position as the last of those anguished sounds
left my mouth.

Nightmare. It isn't real. It isn't real.

I bent over and wrapped my arms around my trembling upper
body as my heart continued to race. As I moved my hands over my
upper arms, I realized that my entire body was drenched in sweat.

I panted as I recalled exactly what had happened in my nightmare.

The sights and sounds of the rebels torturing Mark before he died
had been so damn vivid. So...real.

Tears were streaming down my cheeks as I heard Molly whine
and felt her pawing at my leg.

God, she must have tried to wake me, but I'd been too far gone.

I leaned up so she could climb onto my lap.

"Everything is okay, sweetie," I crooned as I hugged her, savoring
the comforting warmth of her body. "It isn't your fault that you
couldn't wake me up this time."

It was one of the worst nightmares I'd ever experienced.

Still panicked, I reached for my cell phone, and dialed Jax's number without taking time to even think about it.

"Hello," he answered in a sleepy voice.

"You said I could call you anytime," I said breathlessly. "I know it's late, but—"

"Harlow?" He sounded more awake now. "What is it? What the fuck happened?"

I quickly glanced at the clock beside my bed and realized it was almost three o'clock in the morning. "I'm sorry," I said in a shaky voice. "I had a bad dream. I guess I just needed to talk. I just looked at the clock. It's the middle of the night."

"It doesn't matter," he said adamantly, as though he was wide awake now. "Is Molly with you?"

"She's right here," I reassured him. "I'm sure she tried to wake me up, but this nightmare was bad. It was so real. The rebels were torturing Mark. He was in so much pain. The rebel leader ordered his men to cut Mark's fingers off one at a time. There was so much blood, Jax, and I can still hear him screaming. I have to know what happened. I need to know the truth."

"Don't, Harlow," Jax said soothingly. "I promise you, it never happened. There were no signs of any other injuries on his body except for the gunshot that killed him. He didn't suffer. I'm always going to tell you the truth, no matter how difficult that might be."

My body relaxed slightly. "Thank God," I whispered.

I trusted Jax, and I knew he wouldn't lie to me about something like this.

I heard him let out a deep breath before he continued. "We don't know everything that happened with Mark, but we do know that according to the transport boating records, he arrived soon after you and Taylor did. Every statement that Prince Niklaos could get out of the men he arrested were all the same. The rebels only waited long enough for his transport boat to leave the dock before they surrounded him. I doubt that Mark even really understood what was happening before he was killed. I know all of this is difficult to hear, but it was quick, Harlow. He was shot at point-blank range in the head."

I held onto Molly tightly as I processed the information. "Thank you," I said softly into the phone. "Dr. Romero told me that I was going to have to face all the truths of this incident before I could truly heal. I think she's right. The not knowing, and all the avoidance I've done is what's really hurting me. If I don't know the real truth, my imagination can run wild."

"I don't think we'll ever really know more than what I just told you," Jax said gently. "But it happened so fast, I don't think there's anything we really don't know."

"I was out of my mind with worry for every one of those nine days that we didn't see him. It never really occurred to me that he might already be dead. I just assumed that he was being held somewhere else, or that he'd escaped. I also wondered if he'd already been released once my ransom was paid. Not once did I think about the fact that he could have been killed," I explained to Jax in a shaky voice. "I don't know why I didn't consider that option."

"Why would you?" Jax questioned. "The rebels didn't shoot you or Taylor. It was natural to assume he was still alive, Harlow. You needed some kind of hope at that point, so blocking out the worst possible outcome was normal. Once Marshall told you that Mark's body had been found, it's also human nature to go into denial when the truth is more than you can handle."

Raw, relentless pain clawed at my body as I finally processed the fact that Mark was gone, and I was never going to see him again. Maybe I'd acknowledged that on a superficial level before, but I'd never felt the soul-deep loss I was feeling right now. "I couldn't even attend his funeral, Jax," I said on a choked sob. "I never got to say goodbye."

Once the dam had broken, there was no holding back the tears, or the sobs of heartache.

Jax just let me cry, and comforted me with supportive words in his low, reassuring baritone until I slowly calmed down.

"You couldn't go to his service because you were still in the hospital being treated for dehydration, Harlow," Jax said calmly. "It's completely unreasonable to think that you could have made a trip to Mark's hometown in Northern California to attend the service. Even though Mark had moved to San Diego, his brother wanted to have him cremated up north in the town where they grew up. He still lives there. So, it was really a memorial service and not a funeral."

"I still wish I could have been there," I said, my entire body aching with regret.

"It was a nice service, Harlow," Jax said. "Cooper and I attended since Hudson was taking care of Taylor. I sent flowers for you because I knew you'd want that if your brain was fully functional. I also made a donation to Mark's favorite charity in your name. If you want, I can show you pictures of the memory boards, and the flowers I sent for you. I can give you the memorial program, too. I saved them because I knew there might be a day when you wanted to see them."

"I think I'd like that. Thank you. I didn't even realize that you went," I replied, touched by his thoughtfulness and all he'd done for me because I'd been in no position to do it myself. "It's comforting to know there was something there with my name on it, even though I didn't send it myself."

"Cooper and I wanted to go. Mark was our employee, and he died while he was working for us," Jax explained. "Mark's brother understood why you couldn't be there. He said that Mark talked about you a lot, and that he'd been hoping to meet you someday. It wasn't clear whether or not Mark had ever told his brother that there was a romance brewing between the two of you. But Mark obviously talked about you fairly often."

"Mark and I weren't even sure where our relationship was going, so I doubt his brother knew much, either," I explained. "I think we both wanted to see if we could make it into a real romance, and Mark had talked about switching jobs so he could spend more time in San Diego. Honestly, I'm not sure that ever would have happened, even if he hadn't died. He loved his job with Montgomery far too much to give it up, and I wouldn't have wanted him to do that unless it was what he really wanted. I truly don't think he was ready to settle down in one location. His wanderlust and his dedication to Montgomery was way too strong. We flirted. We cared about each other. But I think we would have eventually just settled for being really good friends."

"And you would have been okay with that?" Jax questioned.

I thought about that possibility for a moment before I answered. "Yeah. I would have been okay with it if the romance part wasn't meant to be. If nothing else, Mark restored my faith that there really are good men out there. I would have always been grateful for that, even if it hadn't worked out romantically for us. Maybe I've never wanted to admit it, but I was never quite sure if anything more intimate was in the cards for the two of us. I think I really wanted it to happen because he was such an amazing man, but the chemistry was never quite right. I adored him, and I desperately wanted that to be enough, but all the wishing in the world wouldn't have made him the right guy for me if he wasn't."

"That doesn't negate the fact that you lost someone really important in your life, Harlow," Jax said.

"I know," I replied, feeling calmer now. "I'm sorry I woke you up. I know you go into work early. I just suddenly felt like I needed to know as much as I possibly could about what really happened. It's time for me to deal with it so I can eventually move on. My days of living in denial are over."

I heard Jax release a large breath before he answered, "Unfortunately, this is part of the recovery journey, sweetheart, and I'm damn glad you called me. I would have been really pissed off if I'd found out that you were sitting all alone in the dark, trying to work all this out alone."

"How in the world did I ever end up getting an advisor like you?" I queried softly.

Jax had been infinitely kind, patient, and empathetic. After three weeks in his company every day, I was starting to feel…normal.

He never made me feel like there was something wrong with me, even though I'd been a total emotional mess since the first day we'd spent together.

"I have no idea," Jax said with a chuckle. "But it must have been something really, really bad."

"Stop that," I insisted. "I'm trying to tell you how grateful I am. I'm completely serious. I'm not sure where I would be right now if you hadn't insisted on helping me. I won't pretend it's not still a struggle sometimes, but I don't feel like being some version of my previous self again is impossible anymore."

"It never was impossible, and you never stopped being you," he rumbled. "Don't credit me with how far you've come in the last three weeks. Your progress is all about your strength and your determination, not mine."

I sighed. "Will you ever give yourself credit for the nice things you do?"

"Nah. I don't exactly deserve sainthood. You've only seen my good side. I can be a major dick, too," he drawled.

"I find that doubtful," I told him adamantly.

"You shouldn't," he shot back. "I'm usually an asshole. You just happen to be my Achilles' heel, sweetheart."

I was silent for a moment because I wasn't quite sure how I felt about supposedly being one of Jax Montgomery's vulnerabilities.

"I think you're full of shit," I finally told him. "I know you have a good heart, Jax, even if you don't want anybody to know that."

He groaned. "Please. I feel like you're about to tell me that I'm a really nice guy."

"You *are* a nice guy," I confirmed. "What's wrong with that?"

"Because that's what women say when they don't want to hurt a guy's feelings. If they don't find a guy attractive, they're always a *nice guy*."

"It's completely possible for attractive guys to be really nice, too," I said, defending both his gender and mine. "And I think you're already completely aware that you're one of the hottest men on the planet, Jax Montgomery. Any woman who doesn't see that would have to be completely blind."

"But we weren't talking about *any* woman, Harlow. We were talking about *you*," he said huskily.

My heart somersaulted as I sputtered, "I'm one of those women. I'm not exactly blind."

"Does that mean you were attracted to me when I asked you out two years ago?" he asked smoothly.

Dammit! He'd backed me into a corner without even really trying.

Fine! I was always honest with him, so I answered, "I was attracted to you. When I refused your offer two years ago, it wasn't because I didn't want to get you naked and have hot, sweaty sex with you. Honestly, I even wondered if one night with you might be worth being hounded by the media for weeks. Are you happy now?"

"No," he answered hoarsely. "Then what finally made you refuse?"

I let out an exasperated breath. "I told you that I was at a point in my life where I was looking for more, and you were definitely a one-night guy. I was so attracted to you that you were heartache just waiting to happen. While I had no doubt that the sex would have been amazing, I've never done one-night stands. So I would have ended up feeling like a slut, and I knew I'd see you often enough at the lab that I'd feel even worse. In the end, I wasn't willing to trade my dignity for one night of fleeting carnal pleasure." I took a deep breath before I added, "It's late. We need to go so you can get some sleep."

Oh, God, what had I just said? Yeah, it was the truth, but had I really needed to spill my guts about all that to Jax?

Yeah, maybe I *had* needed to tell him the truth. After everything he'd done for me, he deserved to know why I'd laughed in his face. My bitchiness that day had been nothing but a defense mechanism. I'd been so tempted to take Jax up on his offer that I'd felt like I *had* to drive him away.

No matter how much my opinion of Jax had changed, he was still a one-night guy, and I was a monogamous type of woman.

The seconds ticked by in total silence until Jax finally asked, "Are you going to be okay? What if you can't go back to sleep?"

I breathed a sigh of relief that Jax had obviously decided not to push on the same topic. "I'm fine. Molly is here. I'll get back to sleep. Calling you this late was a knee-jerk reaction because I hadn't given myself the chance to calm down."

"I want you to call me anytime you have a nightmare. Are you being straight with me, Harlow? If you're not okay, I can come over—"

"No!" I said firmly. "If I wasn't okay, I'd tell you. Go back to sleep, Jax."

"Call me back if you can't sleep," he demanded.

"I'll sleep. I feel better knowing that nothing about that nightmare was real. Goodnight, Jax," I murmured.

"Hey, Harlow?" he said in a husky voice.

"Yeah?" I answered.

"Just a couple of things for the record. Number one, I felt the same attraction that you did when we met two years ago. Number two, if you're under the impression that I slept with every woman I dated, I didn't. Number three, I have no idea if we would have ended up sleeping together if we'd had a first date. No doubt my dick would have been hard all damn evening, but I didn't ask you out for a quick fuck. I just wanted to get to know you better. Now that I do know you, I can tell you one more thing..."

I waited, my heart racing as Jax hesitated. "Tell me," I whispered.

"Now that I do know you," he started again, "I can tell you that if you would have said *yes*, there's no way in hell that I would have been satisfied with just one date. Night, Harlow. Get some sleep."

"Night, Jax," I answered in a barely audible voice.

I dropped the phone on the bed and buried my face in Molly's silky fur as I mumbled to her, "Your human daddy is a very confusing man."

She put her snout close to my ear and snuffled, as though she was trying to tell me I was absolutely right.

Chapter 10

Jax

Two nights later, I knocked on Harlow's door a little after our usual meet up time.

Since we were breaking our normal routine, I'd headed home after work to change clothes and to pick up Tango.

"Hi," Harlow said as she smiled at me. "Come on in. I'm almost ready."

Anything I'd meant to say to her had gone flying out of my brain as soon as she'd answered the door.

I shut the door behind me, leaned against it, and watched Harlow as she dashed around the tiny apartment. I couldn't even take my eyes off her as Molly rushed to greet me, and I bent down to give her a hello pat.

"Holy shit! You look beautiful, Harlow," I told her as she put on a second dangly earring that matched the one she was already wearing.

Okay, so *that* wasn't exactly what I'd meant to say, but there had been no way those words *weren't* coming out of my mouth.

She did, in fact, look radiant. Granted, there was never a time when Harlow wasn't smoking hot, but there was something different about her today.

I wasn't sure if it was the black-and-white sweater dress that clung lovingly to every curve of her body, or the black high heels she was wearing with it.

Hell, it could be the fuck-me red lipstick or all the accessorized costume jewelry she was wearing, too.

Most of the time, Harlow didn't wear her hair down, but all those curly blonde locks were streaming over her shoulders and down her back tonight. My fingers were itching to reach out and touch them, but I forced myself not to do it.

"Thanks," she said, sounding a little flustered. "I finally went to get my hair cut and highlighted, and I was able to restock all my makeup. I ran out over a month ago."

I knew I was still staring at her like an idiot, but I couldn't seem to help myself.

"You managed to do all of that today?" I asked.

She snorted. "It wasn't exactly taxing. I told you I was driving again and starting to get out more. I feel like a new woman today. My hair was driving me absolutely insane."

I suddenly realized that the difference in Harlow had nothing to do with her clothes, her shoes, or her hair.

She's getting her confidence back.

And damned if that wasn't one of the sexiest things I'd ever seen.

"How did the day go?" I questioned, reminding myself that I was still her advisor.

"It went really well," she said. "I thought I might get antsy from sitting in the salon for so long, but it actually felt...normal. I guess there's something therapeutic about getting back into some of my old routines. I called Mark's brother this morning. It felt good just to chat with him, and let him know how sorry I was for his loss. He was really nice, and it seemed to help him to talk to someone who knew Mark well as an adult. A lot of people in Mark's hometown hadn't seen him in years. This has to be really hard for him. Mark was his closest family."

I nodded. "I know. Do you think having that conversation helped you, too?"

In my mind, just the fact that Harlow was accepting Mark's death without the crushing guilt she'd previously shouldered was huge progress.

Knowing that she'd reached out to Mark's brother to provide comfort to him was pretty damn amazing.

"It did," she said as she grabbed her jacket and purse from the couch. "It gave me a sense of closure. I'll always miss Mark, but I'm more at peace with myself. I'm ready now."

She shot me a beautiful smile as she stopped beside me, and my heart nearly exploded.

It had only been a little over three weeks since I'd stood near this same door and tried to coax a reluctant, anxious Harlow outside.

Even though I knew she still had some hurdles to get over, it felt so damn good to see Harlow taking her life back again.

"You two behave," I warned Molly and Tango as the two of them played in the small living room.

The dogs had been running around the small apartment since I'd let Tango in behind me.

"I'm glad you brought him over," Harlow said happily. "They miss each other."

"Like I had a choice?" I asked drily as we stepped outside, and Harlow locked the door. "I would have had to put up with an enormous doggie sulk if Tango scented either you or Molly on me when I got home. It's not a pretty sight."

She laughed, and took my hand when I held it out to her. "What rocket ship are you piloting today?"

I grinned as we headed for the parking lot. "You're going to be horribly bored. I brought the Mercedes SUV since we're taking a longer ride. No Bugatti Chiron or Ferrari today."

"So we're only riding in a cheap, six-figure vehicle instead of one that costs way over seven figures. I feel terribly deflated," she said sarcastically.

I chuckled. "Come on. Admit it. You're starting to love the Chiron."

Maybe she wanted to pretend she didn't enjoy the ride, but she squealed with excitement every damn time we accelerated onto the freeway.

"It's a beautiful vehicle, and it's so powerful," she confessed. "I guess it just freaks me out to be riding in a car that costs three million dollars or so."

I opened the passenger side of the SUV for her, and jogged around to the driver's side once she was settled. "Really, none of them are just vehicles," I explained as I got in and started the car. "They're more like...collectibles. A lot of them actually increase in value over time. It's not exactly a waste of money. I do eventually part with the ones that I don't end up driving often, and most of the time, they sell at a profit."

"Didn't anyone ever tell you that you aren't supposed to play with collectibles?" she teased.

I got the SUV in motion, and pulled out of the parking lot. "What's the fun in that?" I asked. "I don't want to buy something that I just put on a shelf and look at every once in a while."

"I have to admit, riding in your rocket ships is a lot more fun," she agreed reluctantly.

"I knew you'd come around," I answered playfully. "So what do you think this whole impromptu get-together at Riley's place is all about? She only gave me a few hours' notice, and not attending wasn't exactly an option."

"I have no idea," Harlow said, sounding equally perplexed. "Taylor was the one who called me and asked me to come."

"At first, I thought that it had to do with Riley," I shared. "I was thinking that maybe she was pregnant, and wanted to tell all of us together. Once I found out that Taylor had asked you to come, I knew that couldn't be it. It has to be something about Taylor and Hudson. It's the only thing that makes sense. Maybe Taylor is pregnant? It really doesn't matter to me which one is having a kid. I'd just like to finally have a niece or nephew."

"Whoa, slow down," Harlow said, her voice filled with humor. "I don't think Taylor is pregnant. She wants to wait until she finishes her doctorate. I could be wrong, but I kind of assume she and Hudson are going to announce that they're getting married."

I thought that over as I merged onto the freeway. "I think Hudson would have told me," I finally concluded. "There isn't much we don't talk about."

"I'm not so sure," Harlow countered. "Don't you think he would have wanted to get a *yes* answer out of Taylor first?"

"You might be right," I grumbled. "In some ways, it kind of sucks that Cooper and I aren't the first to hear about what's happening with Hudson anymore. We've always been really tight."

"Change is always hard," Harlow murmured. "It wasn't easy for you when Riley got married, either, was it?"

"I'm not sure I want to answer that because it may make me sound like a dick, but I will. It was hard because Riley and I used to hang out together. She came to Coronado for the weekends a lot, and we met for dinner in San Diego fairly often. I miss that. But I sure as hell wouldn't want it any other way for her. I was happy for her. Seth was the right guy. She's finally happy, and Riley deserves that. I just miss seeing her more often. It was kind of strange when she first got married, and all of a sudden she was rarely around anymore."

"I'm sure she misses all of you, too," she replied thoughtfully.

"We get together as often as possible now," I told her. "It's not like Citrus Beach is across the country. I guess we just all get busy doing our own things, but Riley never lets too much time pass before she announces one of her get-togethers. Although, we do usually get a lot more notice than this."

"Wouldn't it be fantastic if Hudson and Taylor really are getting married?" she said with a sigh. "At least one amazing thing would come out of the whole kidnapping ordeal."

"I never thought about it that way," I said. "But you're right. I doubt very much if the two of them would have crossed paths any other way."

Granted, Taylor had been a summer intern, but between the headquarters, and the laboratory next door, we had thousands of employees in those two buildings. Hudson rarely popped his head into the lab. Those interests were more up my alley. Hudson was more fixated on the actual mining operations.

"I never ran into a single Montgomery during my internship or as a permanent employee after that," Harlow said. "You were the first one I ever talked to when we ran into each other two years ago in the lab. There's thousands of people at Montgomery who I don't know. I think we science nerds prefer to just hang out with our own teams."

"I saw you around," I admitted. "Not as an intern, but I saw you at the headquarters a few times after you became a team leader. You came over to file your reports."

"I'm surprised you even remembered me," Harlow said thoughtfully.

"You're a very hard woman to forget," I drawled.

Harlow had been a very beautiful blonde in a lab jacket, carrying what had looked like a huge pile of reports.

One, she was gorgeous.

Two, I had a thing for intelligent women.

Put those two things together, and hell yes, I noticed her.

I'd just never had the opportunity to actually have a conversation with her until I'd dropped into the lab that day.

"I still regret the way I treated you when we first met," she said wistfully. "I wish I would have realized that most of the stuff I'd heard about you was utter and complete bullshit."

"Not all of it," I corrected, knowing I really had to set Harlow straight. "There's plenty of shit I've done in my life that I regret. I told you that I didn't sleep with every woman I dated, which is true, but that doesn't mean I've *never* had one-nighters. I was a SEAL. For the most part, the Navy owned me. I watched some of the other guys try to have relationships, wives, kids. There were times when their service to the country had to come before all of those things, and I knew it tore their asses apart. I didn't even consider having any kind of serious relationship when I knew I could be deployed at a moment's notice, but I still wanted to get laid. So yeah, I did my fair share of one-night-only deals if that's what we both wanted."

She sighed. "Was it really that bad if you both agreed to it? The military can be really rough on relationships sometimes, and you were young. You told me you had your college degree by the time you were eighteen, so I'm assuming you went in at the same age I did. I was young and dumb for nearly my entire enlistment, and I did some really stupid things, too."

Jesus! Was there nothing I could tell this woman to make her see that I could be a major asshole?

"I earned my reputation, Harlow. I'm still the king of one-and-done when it comes to dating," I informed her.

"Why?" she asked calmly.

"Why what?"

"Why are you always a one-and-done kind of guy?"

I shrugged. "If it's not there, it's not there. Why prolong the agony? It's not like I wouldn't have loved to find that woman who wanted to be with me more than she wanted to date a billionaire or a Montgomery. It just never happened. Not all of those women were first dates, either. It just so happened that the press never saw me with the same woman twice because none of my relationships lasted for long."

"Dating is all about getting to know someone to see if you fit. There's nothing wrong with looking for a person who clicks with you, even if it takes a while. Why did you keep letting the media write things that made people believe you slept with all those women and just dumped them?" she asked.

"Like I said, occasionally they did turn into one-nighters, or short relationships. And I've been a Montgomery long enough to know that you can't stop the media from painting whatever picture they want. Making me into a playboy who slept with every woman I dated was a lot more interesting to them than the truth. Ultimately, I didn't really give a shit what they wrote about me, and almost every woman I dated thrived on having their time in the spotlight," I muttered.

"Was that before or after they threw up on their shoes?" she asked drily.

I chuckled before I could stop myself. Harlow was almost as sarcastic as I was sometimes. "Most of them didn't have to be drunk to relish being seen with a Montgomery."

"So is that all you've got?" she questioned. "Some one-nighters and short relationships because you dated some of the biggest idiots on the planet?"

"I wasn't exactly in favor of Hudson's relationship with Taylor in the very beginning," I confessed. "I tried to talk him out of taking her home with him."

"Why?" she asked in a surprised tone.

"Because I knew he felt guilty about what happened because she was there for Montgomery. I thought he was motivated by guilt, and I didn't want him to get in over his head. I backed off once I realized he actually had feelings for her other than guilt, but I was an asshole. I should have known he wasn't going to pass her care on to someone else, even during the rescue. It was a long damn hike back to the coast from the rebel camp, and he never once let me carry Taylor. I took both our packs, but he was insistent that he didn't want her to wake up and not recognize who was carrying her."

"How bad was it, really?" Harlow asked earnestly.

I wasn't even going to pretend like I didn't know what she was asking. "It was bad. I wasn't even sure she'd live until we got her to the coast. It was a fucking miracle she still had a heartbeat when we got there. I don't know how you two survived in that little shithole. It was sweltering when we broke in to get to Taylor, and it was the middle of the damn night. Under any circumstance Hudson and I could think of, Taylor was already dead from dehydration, but we had to try. Even if all we could do for her was bring her body home."

"I knew it was bad," Harlow said in a tremulous voice. "But Taylor downplayed it as much as possible. Thank you for telling me the truth."

Oh, hell, maybe I shouldn't have told her. I hated hearing her upset. "She made it, Harlow. That's all that really matters. Once we were able to get fluids into her, we knew she was going to make it home."

"So if they are getting married, I take it you'd approve now," Harlow said.

"Hell, yes," I said firmly. "Hudson would be wrecked without her, and Taylor sees him like no other woman ever has before. The two of them belong together."

"I think you're right," Harlow agreed with a sigh.

Okay, so much for trying to get her to see what a dick I could be sometimes.

I wasn't even sure why I'd felt the need to try in the first place.

Maybe I was trying to get her to alter her opinion about me so I could put a little bit of distance between the two of us.

Ever since she'd broken down and told me why she'd turned me down two years ago, all I could think about was the fact that she'd been attracted to me back then. If it hadn't been for my crappy reputation, Harlow and I could have started dating two years ago.

I tried not to dwell on something that had never happened. Circumstances had changed, and the last thing Harlow needed from me right now was to alter our friendship in any way.

She needed more time.

She needed to feel normal.

What she *didn't* need was anything that was going to throw her off-balance when she was just learning to stand on her own two feet again.

If I really wanted things to be different with Harlow in the future, I was going to have to settle my ass down and be patient.

Problem was, as she became less vulnerable, and more like the vivacious, brilliant woman I'd met two years ago, the waiting got more torturous every single day.

"Jax?" Harlow murmured.

"Yeah?"

Harlow released an audible breath. "You can tell Hudson you're my advisor now. I'm going to tell Taylor. I think she and I need to talk. I think I'm ready now."

Thank fuck!

I really needed my older brother's advice to figure out how I was going to live through another damn day without trying to seduce Harlow.

Chapter 11

Harlow

"I'm so happy for you," I told Taylor as I hugged her tightly. The big news had been exactly what I'd thought it would be.

Hudson and Taylor were now engaged, and the diamond engagement ring she was sporting on her left hand was absolutely stunning.

The gathering had been a small, informal dinner. Hudson, Jax, Cooper, Taylor, and I had been the only invited guests.

Riley had hauled Taylor and me into the living room after dinner, and told the men to go do something so we could indulge in some girl talk about the wedding.

Seated on the couch beside Taylor, I held onto her a little longer than necessary for a happy hug. Knowing just how close I'd come to losing her, it wasn't easy to let her go.

"I was ecstatic when I found out," Riley said from her seat in a comfy recliner near the sofa.

Riley's comment finally prompted me to let go of my death grip on Taylor so she could breathe.

I'd liked Riley from the moment we'd been introduced. I almost felt like I knew her already since Jax talked about all of his siblings a lot.

I gave Taylor a little space, and picked up the glass of wine Riley had given me.

"So when is the big day?" I asked.

"Sometime next year. Late summer or early fall. We haven't set an exact date yet," Taylor answered. "We're already living together, and we're both completely committed, so we'll give ourselves time to get everything together for the wedding. Hudson is so busy, and I'm working and getting ready to start my doctorate. There's no real reason to rush."

Riley laughed. "Hudson will be really antsy to tie the knot by then, but I'm glad we have time to plan."

"Harlow, will you be my maid of honor?" Taylor asked excitedly.

I almost choked on my wine. "Me? What about Riley or one of your friends from Stanford?"

Taylor's eyes widened. "Do you really have to ask that question after all we've been through? I'm not even really in contact with my friends up north anymore. Most of the casual friends I had there have finished their degrees and don't even live there anymore. And Riley is going to be a bridesmaid. Jax is going to be the best man, and Seth will be standing up for Hudson, too. Cooper already agreed to walk me down the aisle. You're my closest friend, Harlow."

Tears welled up in my eyes as I looked at Taylor's sincere expression.

Truthfully, Taylor was my closest friend, too, and I wasn't happy that I'd distanced myself from her simply because of my guilt.

We chatted a few times a week on the phone, so it wasn't like we'd completely lost touch, but I'd refused every suggestion she'd made to get together in person. I hadn't wanted her to know that I was struggling because she'd had such a full plate herself.

"I'd be completely honored, Taylor," I replied earnestly as I looked from Taylor to Riley. "I think I'm going to need some help from the bridesmaid. I've actually never been in a wedding party before."

Riley waved her hand in the air like it was no big deal. "I've got you covered, Harlow. I grew up a Montgomery. If I learned nothing else from my mother, she did teach me how to organize large events. I both planned and attended ridiculously lavish parties before I separated myself from the social elite crowd. I've taken part in some pretty elaborate weddings, too. We'll make sure that Taylor has the wedding of her dreams."

I took a sip of wine, feeling a little more relaxed. "Will your mother be at the wedding? I hate to be ignorant, but Jax has never said a thing about his mother. I know that your dad died a long time ago."

I could feel the tension in the air as Riley and Taylor exchanged an awkward look.

"I noticed you came here with Jax," Riley observed. "Do you two talk often?"

Crap! Maybe I shouldn't have mentioned Jax.

Honestly, there was no reason why I couldn't tell them that Jax and I had become friends, but I had to watch what I said since Riley was in the dark about the existence of Last Hope. Jax and his brothers had decided not to tell their little sister about the organization because they were afraid she'd worry.

I could reveal things from a Montgomery Mining angle, but nothing that would tip Riley off about how Taylor was rescued, or her brother's personal involvement in that mission.

I took a deep breath before I answered. "We spend a lot of time together. I was having some coping issues after the kidnapping incident. I lost someone I cared about on our work team."

Riley nodded. "Hudson told me that he lost an employee. He was devastated. Were you close?"

"Yes. I guess you could say he was my boyfriend, but we really never got the time to figure out if the relationship was going anywhere. We were close friends, though."

Riley's expression was empathetic as she replied, "Oh, my God, Harlow. I'm so sorry. It would have been difficult enough to deal with the emotional trauma of what happened to you and Taylor. I can't imagine losing someone close to you because of that incident, too."

"It was hard," I confessed. "But I'm doing better. Jax has helped me a lot. Once I got back to San Diego after doing my initial recovery at my mom's place in Carlsbad, Jax stopped by to see how I was doing. We've been friends ever since. He's been really supportive. Your brother is a good man."

That's about the best I can do without coughing up details.

"It's about time that another woman noticed that," Riley said. "I've known it for as long as I can remember. His playboy reputation is ridiculous."

I smiled. "It didn't take me all that long to figure that out. I just wished I'd known it two years ago when he asked me out to dinner. I turned him down flat because of that reputation, but I didn't know him back then like I do now."

Riley's eyes widened. "You actually turned down a date with Jax?"

"You never told me about that, Harlow," Taylor admonished.

"It was nothing, really," I said self-consciously. "One minute we were discussing soil samples, and the next he was asking me out to dinner. I doubt there are very many women who aren't aware of his reputation, so I refused. Looking back, I wish I hadn't rushed to judgment just because of the gossip. I'm not usually so easily swayed, but I didn't want to be hounded by the media just because I'd been one of Jax's one-off dates."

Riley shot me a questioning look. "I highly doubt that would have happened. Jax hasn't exactly met a lot of quality women. He was rarely in one place long enough to have a meaningful relationship when he was in the Navy, and when he came back, the only females he mingled with were clubbers or women from our old social circle. Normally, he never would have dated someone who worked for him. He always said since he was the boss, he didn't feel comfortable doing that. He must have *really* liked you to make an exception, but I completely understand why you refused."

I could feel my face turning warm, and I knew I was blushing. "It all worked out," I said in a rush, wanting to change the topic. "I'm grateful for everything he's done for me."

"Except for the settlement offer," Taylor said with a laugh. "I know you had the same reaction I did about that."

I rolled my eyes. "It was absolutely ridiculous to think Montgomery needed to fill up my bank account for something that wasn't even their fault. They negotiated my ransom, paid it, and got me out of there alive. After I got back, they took care of everything, including every single bill I incurred because of the incident."

"Usually, money fixes everything for my brothers," Riley mused. "Most people would have scooped up that offer in a heartbeat, even if Montgomery wasn't really at fault."

"They did nothing wrong. It was a routine expedition in a country known to be safe for visitors. The odds of something like a kidnapping taking place are astronomical." I smiled. "Jax was pretty persistent about it, and so was the legal department, probably because he asked them to hound me."

Riley snorted. "None of my brothers give up easily. Unfortunately, they're very used to getting their way. It was good for them to finally have you and Taylor tell them no."

"After I turned down a date with Jax, and considering my refusal to take his money, I'm surprised he showed up on my doorstep, but I'm glad he did," I told them. "I think I needed an objective friend who wasn't struggling with the same issues I was at the time."

"Have you been to his place in Coronado?" Riley asked.

I hesitated, but since I'd already slipped up by telling them about what happened two years ago, I didn't think admitting I'd been to his house was a big deal.

I nodded. "Yes. It's an incredible home. I love it there. It can be touristy, but the off-season is really nice. I'm glad you reminded me of Coronado. I've been using your bike. I hope you don't mind."

"Of course I don't," Riley assured me. "And it wasn't really mine. Jax bought it for me to use when I was there. I got myself a similar one to use here. They ride like a dream. I really miss getting there more often. And just FYI...I don't think Jax has ever taken a woman to his place."

"I'm not one of his women," I rushed to explain. "I'm just his friend."

Riley crossed her arms over her chest. "Really? Jax looks at you like he's starving, and you're the first item on his dinner menu. Come on, Harlow. I know my brothers, and I've already seen that look on Hudson's face when he looks at Taylor."

"I noticed it, too," Taylor added. "I didn't know you guys had hooked up, but it's perfectly obvious that he's attracted to you."

I shook my head. "Maybe he was two years ago, but he's never done a single thing since we've been friends to make me think that the attraction is still there. Honestly, he's just been an amazing support system for me, and keeping his dog Molly with me has really helped."

"He actually gave Molly to you?" Riley asked in a shocked voice.

"Not forever," I assured her. "She's just on loan for a while."

"Jax adores Tango and Molly. He rarely lets them out of his sight. He doesn't loan his dogs," Riley said. "Now I'm convinced he's got it bad for you."

"He told me he loans Molly out sometimes," I argued.

"He lied," Riley shot back. "But in his defense, he probably did it so you'd feel more comfortable. Parting with one of his dogs, even for a short time, would kill Jax. He'd never trust someone else to make sure Molly was well taken care of and safe. She was a shelter dog, and she was abused as a puppy. Not that anybody would know that because she's so loving now, but Jax wouldn't take the chance of that ever happening again. That's why he kept her. He loaned her to you because he trusts you."

"He never told me," I muttered.

"Don't be mad," Riley pleaded.

"I'm not," I replied. "Not at all. I know he meant well."

I couldn't bring myself to get angry because Jax had lied. I knew he'd been trying to make me comfortable.

Knowing the truth made me want to cry because he'd gone out on a limb with Molly's safety just to help me.

I blinked back my tears as I said, "I think Jax is probably the most incredible guy I've ever known. The sad part is, I don't think he knows just how amazing he really is, or how much some of the things he does helps other people. He keeps pointing out all of his faults, like I'm supposed to suddenly be turned off because of them. God, we all have flaws, but doesn't he realize that all of the good things he does far outweighs the bad?"

"No," Riley replied morosely. "All of my brothers are ridiculously critical of themselves. You asked about my mother, and I'm ready to answer that question now that I know how much you care about Jax."

My heart started to race as I waited for her to continue.

Chapter 12

Harlow

"My mother is alive," Riley said solemnly. "But there's no way in hell she'll ever be attending any of her children's weddings. Jax would never tell you that my father molested me as a child for many years. All of my brothers respect my privacy, but I think it's important for any woman who cares about one of my brothers to know what our childhood was like. My mother knew what my father was doing, and she was actually his enabler rather than my protector. The status of the Montgomery name is everything to her, and the last thing she wanted was that kind of blemish or rumor to tarnish it. God forbid she couldn't reign over the social elite crowd anymore. So she covered it up in any way she could. The woman is pure evil, just like my father."

I was stunned, so it took me a few moments before I said, "The only thing Jax has ever told me is that his parents were monsters. I'm so sorry you had to go through that, Riley."

"Thanks," she answered. "It screwed with my head for a long time, but it doesn't anymore. Good treatment and an incredibly supportive husband helped me get past all that, but I think our childhood still left a mark on my brothers. They never knew it was happening, and I was too ashamed to tell them about it until long after my father was dead. None of them had it very easy, either. To be honest, none of us really had a childhood. My brothers were all shipped off to a boarding school for the intellectually gifted at a young age, and my father expected perfection. They were Montgomery heirs, and nothing was ever good enough. For God's sake, the man had three sons who were geniuses, and that wasn't good enough for him. We were all like Stepford children who wouldn't dare do one tiny thing out of line. Yet, when the boys were home on vacation or breaks, they got nothing but criticism, and my parents were brutal in their cruelty. So yeah, that eventually rubbed off on all of them to the point where they criticized themselves the same way."

"It was really bad," Taylor added. "Hudson gets bogged down in guilt, and I think Jax still has issues seeing anything really good about himself. The arrogance is self-defense. All three of them can be high-handed and bossy, but I know in Hudson's case, it's nothing more than his concern about my wellbeing."

Riley nodded. "All of them put on a good pretense on the exterior. I doubt most people see anything other than their fierce business acumen, and their confidence. Inside, it's a different story. Every single one of them still tries to live up to impossibly high expectations, but feels like they fall short. It was probably a blessing that every single one of them went into the military. I think they found a purpose to their lives that they didn't have before, and they escaped from my father's influence."

I shuddered as I thought about the childhood of constant criticism and emotional cruelty that Jax had endured. "Do you think they're happy running Montgomery?"

"Absolutely," Riley responded. "My brothers have pushed Montgomery to heights that it never saw under my father's management. What better way to reassure themselves that they're smarter than he was? They've all achieved their own success, and done things their way. Unfortunately, those childhood insecurities have a way of creeping back into the psyche sometimes. Lord knows we never heard a kind word or praise growing up. So we can all be hypercritical of ourselves sometimes. I'm not sure that instinct ever completely goes away."

I shook my head. "I had no idea how bad it was, and I'm sure they blame themselves for what happened to you, even though they shouldn't."

"Of course they do," Riley confirmed. "They're my big brothers. They think they should have been able to keep me away from anybody and anything that would hurt me. I'm not sure any of them realize that they aren't superhuman."

"Their protective instinct is definitely in overdrive most of the time," Taylor added.

Riley chuckled. "While I can't vouch for that from a romantic point of view, the three of them can be overbearingly protective of me as their little sister."

I smiled. "I've heard that. I think Jax said that all of them threatened to cut Seth's balls off if he hurt you."

"Oh, they did," Riley said in an amused tone. "Luckily, my husband doesn't back down easily, and he's just as protective as my brothers are, so they understood each other."

"Does all of that protectiveness drive you crazy?" I asked curiously.

"No," Riley and Taylor answered in unison.

My smile widened. "I guess the cavemen win."

Taylor smiled back at me. "I don't think it bothers either one of us because Riley and I both know how to stand up for ourselves when Hudson or Seth are being completely unreasonable. When they aren't, it's kind of nice to know they're making our wellbeing their priority. It's kind of hard not to find it endearing when they get all grumpy on our behalf. It's actually kind of hot." She paused before she added, "Sorry, Riley—that's probably TMI since Hudson is your brother."

"It's not like I don't know that my brothers are handsome beasts," she said lightly. "Just try not to get too nauseating."

I listened to Riley and Taylor banter back and forth for a few minutes while I tried to process the information Riley had given me.

Knowing Jax's background, it was easy to put the puzzle pieces together now.

Underneath that smart-ass exterior of his, he wanted the same thing everybody else craved.

Love.

Acceptance.

Understanding.

Warmth.

And all of the other things he'd never gotten as a child.

Yeah, he was a confident guy, and for the most part, he had his shit together.

However, I had a feeling all the serial, one-off dating he'd done really was a search for something or someone.

I found it heartbreaking that, after all this time, Jax Montgomery had never found someone who could see into his heart instead of just his very large wallet.

"I vote for jewel tone or black dresses. What do you think, Harlow?" Riley asked.

I snapped out of my musings when I heard my name. "I'm sorry. I think I missed what you said," I confessed.

"I was just telling Taylor I'd have to hurt her if she makes me wear some pink, puffy marshmallow dress. Since I'm a redhead, and you're a blonde, I think black or jewel colors would work for both of us. Most pastels clash with my hair."

I smiled. "I think either would be great. Maybe black because it keeps things classy, and most of the attention on the bride where it belongs."

"I doubt I'll end up in bright white," Taylor said. "Since I'm a redhead, too, I think traditional white might wash me out. I might go more ivory."

"I think you should try on a bunch of different shades," Riley suggested.

"I think so, too," I added. "It's hard to tell what will work until you see it on."

"We have plenty of time," Taylor said. "I'm not all that fond of clothes shopping, but I'll do it when I have to. I guess I can't order a bridal dress online."

"Absolutely not," Riley affirmed. "We'll make a day of it. We'll find a date that works for all of us, and Harlow and I will find a way to make it less painful. Maybe a nice brunch somewhere would help."

The living room was silent for a moment as Riley and Taylor both drank a little of their wine.

"Thank you for sharing what happened to you, Riley," I said, breaking the silence. "Knowing how Jax grew up helps me make sense out of some of the things he says sometimes."

Riley swallowed before she answered, "Don't even let that non-chalant, sarcastic, jokester attitude fool you. Jax has a heart of gold. He just rarely lets anyone see it."

"I'm starting to get that now," I told her. "It's kind of interesting that from the outside, I'm sure it looked like you were the family who had it all."

"Sometimes those are the families who are the most dysfunctional," Riley said with a sad smile.

I nodded slowly. "I guess I was really lucky. I lost my dad when I was in high school, but both of my parents were always supportive, and I always knew it when they were proud of me. We didn't have a lot of money, and things were really tight after my father died, but Mom was and is my rock. She's been there to cheer for every one of my successes, and pull me up from every failure."

"God, she must have been frantic when you were kidnapped," Riley pondered.

"She was, and I felt so guilty that I didn't want to share that I was struggling to cope with what happened. That's why I'm so grateful to Jax. I can tell him almost anything and he never judges. He helped me feel normal again," I shared.

Taylor reached out and took my hand. "I would have been there for you, Harlow. You never told me you were really having a hard time."

"I know," I said as I squeezed her hand before I released it. "But you were recovering, too. I didn't want to bring you down."

"You wouldn't have brought me down, but I'm glad you had Jax," she said earnestly.

"Me, too," Riley added. "And don't believe for a single minute that he's not still attracted to you. I think maybe he's trying to give you time to heal by just being supportive. I think the question is, are you attracted to him? You obviously turned down the opportunity to go out with him. Was it just his player reputation, or was the interest just not there?"

I sighed. "Seriously? Jax is ridiculously attractive, intelligent, successful, and he has a wicked sense of humor. How could any woman not be attracted to him? He draws women to him without even trying. When I'm with him, women check him out more than once, even if they don't recognize him as a Montgomery."

"You are still attracted to him if you notice *that*," Taylor said with a chuckle.

"I am. I won't deny it. I was attracted to him when he asked me out, and I still am, but we're just friends. Maybe you two don't believe it's just friendship, but I have no delusions that Jax Montgomery wants to get one of his research geoscientists naked."

"Ha! Little do you know," Riley teased. "Jax likes intelligent women, and have you looked in the mirror lately? You're beautiful, Harlow. Why wouldn't he still be attracted? Honestly, I've never seen him look at any female the way he looks at you."

"He's a concerned friend," I said adamantly.

"Who just happens to be undressing you with his eyes?" Taylor asked saucily.

I shook my head, ready to give up. "Stop. If I really thought he was attracted to me, I'd probably break my own rules and offer him a wild fling. Our dating opportunities are gone, but I value him a lot as a friend."

Riley smirked. "You do realize that Taylor and I will be the first ones to say 'I told you so' when he starts pursuing you like a madman."

"Feel free," I told her. "It's not going to happen."

"We'll see," Riley said knowingly. "I think we all need more wine, and I need to hit the bathroom and see how the guys are doing. I'll be back in a while."

"I'm going to take Harlow outside to show her the patio," Taylor called after Riley's retreating figure.

The moment Riley had left the room, Taylor pulled me off the couch and led me out to the patio.

We were barely seated in two side-by-side patio chairs before she said, "When did this start with Jax? I know you're leaving something out, Harlow. Spill it. I want the *entire* story."

Chapter 13

Harlow

"How did you know? Do you think Riley knows, too?" I asked Taylor anxiously.

The light was dimmer outside, but there were enough lights on that I could see her face.

Thankfully, she'd seated us underneath some sort of hot coiled heater that was running near the ceiling, so we were warm, even though it was getting cooler and breezier.

"She doesn't have a clue," Taylor told me. "But I know you, Harlow. I could tell that something was missing, and I have a feeling you're not telling the whole story because of Last Hope."

I quickly gave her an abbreviated version of Jax's role as my advisor, and the agreement I'd made with both him and Marshall.

"But everything else is true," I finished. "We *have* become friends, Taylor. Just like I said."

Taylor's eyes welled up with tears. "Why didn't you tell me what was happening? You always said you were doing okay. I hate that you were practically homebound because of your anxiety and nightmares, and I didn't know. I was giving you your space, but I should have pushed harder. I knew you were grieving Mark."

"Don't," I pleaded with her. "Don't try to pretend that my situation was worse because I lost someone I cared about. Jax told me how close you were to death, Taylor, and I know how damn lucky I am that you're still here with me. Let's be honest about what happened to you when you were pulled out of our holding area every night, too. You were assaulted every single time, weren't you? Please tell me the truth."

This wasn't exactly the way I'd planned on talking to Taylor, but I had to know.

She looked me in the eyes as she said, "Yes. You were out of your mind with worry about Mark, and it wasn't like there was anything you could do if you *had* known the truth."

"Did you lie to protect me?" I asked tearfully.

"I did, and I'd do it again," she said defiantly. "I didn't know that Mark was dead, but the possibility crossed my mind. You were carrying a heavy burden, and I was going to end up getting raped anyway. So I told them that I wouldn't fight it if they left you alone."

"You made a deal with them to save me?"

"It wasn't a sacrifice, Harlow, but if they were going to touch me, I was going to get something out of it."

"How many?" I asked shakily.

"Just the rebel leader," she answered. "He had some kind of hate relationship with my red hair. It *was* going to be *me*, Harlow. You couldn't have stopped it. I also knew I couldn't get pregnant because I had an IUD. Were you protected?"

I shook my head, still in shock. "I'd missed way too many pills to still be protected."

"I thought so. At least I was protected. I figured you weren't."

"With everything else we were going through, how did you bear it?" I asked with a sob.

Taylor scooted forward and took my hands. "Listen to me, Harlow. I got through it, just like you got through your fear and desperation about what had happened to Mark. We did whatever we had to do to survive. And we're both still here. We're both still alive. I'm grateful for that every single day. I ended up getting incredible joy from all that pain and suffering. If it hadn't happened, I never would have met and fell in love with Hudson. You know I practice tai chi, and have since I was a teenager. I've developed a lot of mental discipline because of it. They violated my body, but I never let them win. I zoned out every time it started, and went to a happier place and time. That bastard never touched my mind or my soul. I wouldn't allow it."

Tears poured down my cheeks as I said, "You're so damn brave, Taylor, and so strong."

"So are you, Harlow. You just don't see it. I don't know how you got through nine days of not knowing what happened to someone you cared about. I was hardly acquainted with Mark, and I was worried. He was important to you. And in the end, you lost him anyway. The pain of that loss had to have been crushing. Yet, you still survived. Actually, you sound better than you have for a long time."

"Jax really has helped me. He literally pulled me out of the hell I was making for myself," I explained.

I told Taylor about why I had Molly, my EMDR, and my intensive counseling sessions.

"I'm finally getting over most of my guilt," I said. "I was ready to hear what really happened to you. I had to know the reality versus what I'd made up in my head."

Taylor released my hands and leaned back in her chair. "I'm being completely honest with you, Harlow. I swear. It was just as unpleasant as all the other things we endured, but if we let those bastards mess with our heads any longer, they win. I don't know about you, but I refuse to let them take one more second of my life from me. I'm over it. I'll always be sorry we lost Mark, but I know he'd hate it if we let them win, too. God, I know you miss him, Harlow."

I nodded. "I do, but you're right. I think the best tribute we can give him is to live happy because his opportunity to do that was cut short. He would want that." I took a deep breath before I said, "I don't know where my relationship with him would have gone if he hadn't died, but I don't think that strong emotional pull was really there for either one of us. No matter what, I think we would have always been good friends, though."

Taylor sighed. "Please don't suffer any more guilt about any of this, Harlow, and certainly not about what happened to me. The whole incident was hard for both of us in different ways. We were three innocent victims who were just in the wrong place at the wrong time. The only thing I want for you right now is some peace and happiness. I'm glad Jax has helped you move forward, but please don't shut me out anymore. If you do, I'll come camp out on your doorstep until you let me in."

I shot her a weak smile. "I'm not sure what to say about the bargain you made with the rebel leader. You saved me from having to go through the trauma of sexual assault, and possibly a nightmare pregnancy, too."

"That bargain cost me nothing," she reminded me. "No indignity that I wasn't already going to suffer. I love you, Harlow. You're like the sister I never had. Don't tell me you wouldn't do the same thing if you were in my situation, because I know you would. I already know that if you could have managed it, you would have sent me out of harm's way and stayed behind in that hellhole."

"I would have done anything to have you go instead of me," I rasped.

She smiled. "That's just what real friends do. It's hard to watch someone you care about suffer. You're an amazing woman, Harlow. Don't ever forget that."

I swiped at the tears on my face. "So are you."

"Now, tell me about Jax," she insisted curiously. "There's more than just a friendship there, right?"

"There isn't. I swear."

"Shit!" Taylor cursed. "I thought you were just hiding the juicy details because Riley is his sister. Are you seriously telling me you haven't gotten down and dirty with Jax Montgomery? I'm not attracted to him because I've got the gorgeous love of my life, but Jax is seriously hot."

"I know," I answered. "It seems like I'm noticing that more and more every day. It's like my female hormones are returning with a vengeance. I watch him work out every single day, and the man punishes himself to keep that amazing body of his that fit. It's kind of unfair that he's also gorgeous, and filthy rich."

Taylor chortled. "That's exactly what I used to think about Hudson. If Jax isn't making a move, I say you seduce him. I'm sure your libido was low because you were still trying to get over your trauma and Mark's death. But if Jax melts your panties, go after it."

I chuckled. "Taylor," I admonished. "When did you start turning into a sex maniac?"

Taylor had never been the kind of woman who really talked about men or sex very much. She was pretty low-key.

She wiggled her eyebrows. "Not long after I met Hudson Montgomery. That man completely ruined me. I used to sit at the breakfast bar while he was cooking just to stare at his ass. I swore I could bounce a quarter off that tight butt and it would go flying for miles. I was way too weak to actually do anything about it at the time, but I watched him like a creepy stalker."

I started to laugh so hard that I couldn't stop.

Taylor was hilarious about her fascination with Hudson, and she seemed so damn happy.

"Honestly, Harlow," Taylor said when I finally stopped laughing. "Could you have ever seen a woman like me being the love of Hudson Montgomery's life?"

I raised a brow. "Why not? I think he got lucky."

She rolled her eyes. "He gets lucky all the time. I guess what I'm saying is that it's just so unlikely. I was a poor orphan kid with a face full of freckles and funky glasses. I was an ugly child, and I definitely didn't turn into a beautiful swan as an adult, either." She picked up a lock of hair and held it up. "Same crazy red hair, same unremarkable appearance, same freckles, except they've faded out quite a bit. Hudson looks at me like I'm the most desirable woman on the planet. On the surface, we just don't fit, but for some reason, we do click perfectly. So please don't tell me that Jax can't possibly be attracted to a gorgeous blonde like you."

"He's never even shot me a vague sexual innuendo," I told her.

"Maybe not. But Jax looks at you just like Hudson looks at me. The attraction is there. He's either hesitant because you already turned him down, or because he doesn't think you're ready for anything except friendship. Are you ready for something else?"

"I don't know," I said with a moan. "I told him that I was attracted to him when he asked me out two years ago, and he said he felt the same way, but things change."

"Does he know you still want to get him naked?" she asked.

"I never mentioned it," I said.

"Maybe you should," Taylor suggested. "If you're not ready for anything more, just take it day by day."

"You know I'm a cautious planner," I reminded Taylor.

"There's no harm in doing something different," she mused.

"You're right," I admitted. "I find myself leaning more toward living in the moment because we sure as hell know that tomorrow isn't a guarantee."

"I totally get that," Taylor agreed. "I don't think you can go through a near-death experience, and not have it change the way you look at your life. It's not like you have to let it change your entire personality, but maybe it opens up more possibilities."

I knew what she meant.

Maybe like…blowing a bunch of money on an expensive restaurant just to see if it was as good as its reviews?

Or like…occasionally doing something frivolous for an entire day just because it's fun or relaxing.

Or like…riding in a three-million-dollar vehicle, and openly laughing and enjoying the power of a car that could plaster my body against the seat when it accelerated.

Better yet, asking Jax if I could drive it just for that once-in-a-lifetime experience.

Really, it was just a matter of embracing life, and starting to get all the joy I could from it.

"You're right," I told Taylor. "There's no reason I have to be quite so anal."

"You're responsible, not anal, and there's nothing wrong with that, but you could slack off every once in a while," she teased.

I raised a brow. "I've been slacking for months now. It's driving me insane."

"I really hope that you come back to Montgomery when you're ready. Everybody misses you. You're an incredible team leader. It's not the same there without you," Taylor informed me.

"I might," I said with a shrug. "It is my dream job. I just need to make sure I have my head on straight."

"Take all the time you need," Taylor insisted. "You've worked your ass off your entire life, Harlow. Now that you're starting to feel better, use the time off to recharge and take care of yourself."

"God, I've already been on the payroll without working for a long time," I said with a groan.

"Hudson said it's just a leave of absence."

"I actually resigned, but Hudson and Jax seem to have ignored that resignation. So I am technically on leave. I'm actually glad they did that. I wasn't in my right mind when I quit," I said, owning up to my mistake.

"I think they knew that," Taylor said quietly. "That's why they ignored that resignation. They kept me on the payroll, too. Let them do this for you. It's nothing compared to the settlement they offered."

"I'll talk to Jax about it."

Taylor didn't have a chance to reply because her fiancé came walking out the patio door. "Are you ladies talking about us?" Hudson boomed.

Jax came out right behind him.

Taylor snorted. "Do you really think I have nothing else to talk about except you, Hudson Montgomery?"

He winked at his fiancée. "No. Just wishful thinking. Are we interrupting? I thought you might be ready to head home."

Taylor rose, and Hudson immediately wrapped an arm around her. The move was so natural that it looked like he didn't even have to think about doing it.

I loved watching them together. It was like the two of them could never be close enough.

"You ready to take off?" Jax asked as he automatically took my hand.

My heart started to dance as I realized how instinctive it was for Jax to reach out for me the second we were together. It wasn't like I really needed him to hold my hand anymore.

Or maybe...it's just gotten to be a habit.

"Whenever you are," I told him with a smile. "I just want to thank Riley for inviting me, and for dinner."

"Let's go find her then," Jax suggested as his eyes roamed over me with a hint of possessiveness I'd never seen before. "I think she's yakking with Seth and Cooper."

As we followed Hudson and Taylor into the house, Taylor turned around and gave me an I-saw-the-way-he-looked-at-you wink.

Maybe it hadn't meant a damn thing, but my heart was racing, because I'd finally seen the way he looked at me, too.

Chapter 14

Jax

I waited as Harlow said goodbye to my sister, Cooper, and Seth. Hudson and Taylor had slipped out before we had, and I really regretted not grabbing my older brother so we could have a private conversation.

I needed somebody to knock some sense into my head, and it had better happen soon.

One smile from Harlow had been all it took to get my dick as hard as a rock on the patio, and it still wasn't deflating.

Yeah, I'd had *some* respite when Hudson, Cooper, Seth, and I had retreated to Seth's office to let the ladies have their girl time. Unfortunately, it hadn't been nearly long enough.

I'd started watching Harlow at the beginning of the evening, and I hadn't been able to stop following her every move since.

It wasn't like I hadn't always been attracted to her, but suddenly, it was like someone had flicked the switch on a light inside of Harlow. The way she moved, the way she talked, the way she seemed completely at peace inside her own body…all of it was fucking fascinating.

Her warmth and natural charm had won my sister over almost immediately, and Riley was a little cautious most of the time.

Hell, even Cooper had been reasonably nice to her. Well, as nice as his ornery ass could get these days.

I rubbed the tight muscles at the back of my neck, feeling edgy as hell.

Every damn technique I'd been using for almost a month to keep Harlow in the friend zone didn't seem to be working tonight.

Maybe because she didn't really need me as a support system anymore.

She was smiling.

She was relaxed.

She was confident.

She was perfectly capable of doing almost anything on her own.

And she was back into her old routines.

This was the real Harlow, and she was fucking captivating.

Honestly, I knew none of this change was exactly sudden. Harlow had made progress every single day for nearly a month. More than likely, it was *me* who had suddenly changed and not *her*.

My biggest defense had always been Harlow's vulnerability, and the fact that I was her advisor. What kind of asshole would hit on a woman when she was down? Not me. Not when she needed me to be there for her, and help her get back on her feet.

Because things had happened slowly, it had been easy to ignore that every single day, Harlow had gotten closer to finding her independence again. She'd inched away from me until I really couldn't see the woman who'd been so crippled with fear and anxiety that she never left her apartment.

It wasn't that things weren't going exactly the way I'd hoped, and even faster than I'd anticipated. After the random nightmare that Harlow had experienced about Mark, she hadn't had another one of those, either.

I wasn't going to bullshit myself into believing she was *never* going to feel some residual effects from being a hostage. Nor was she even close to finished with her treatment.

But holy fuck! She was obviously taking her life back, and she wasn't going to need an advisor anymore. That fact was suddenly giving my mind and body other ideas about what roles I could play in this woman's life. Unfortunately, almost all of them should remain off-limits for now.

Still, my mind had been going *there* all evening, off-limits or not.

Problem was that I couldn't rein those thoughts in anymore. It was like the door had burst open, releasing every salacious fantasy I'd ever had about Harlow, and there was no possible way to slam it closed again.

At one point during dinner, I'd gotten so engrossed in thought while I was staring at Harlow that Cooper had elbowed me and said, "Give it a rest, man. You're going to freak her out if you keep looking at her like she's dessert."

That warning had curtailed my compulsion for all of five minutes before my gaze automatically went back to Harlow.

Fuck! My obsession kind of reminded me of one of those idiots who gets so mesmerized by a natural disaster that they forget to move the hell out of the way. They know that shit is coming to kill them, but they're still totally absorbed with watching it.

Yeah, as a matter of fact, it *was* just like that, except I was that idiot this time.

Harlow squeezed my hand, and it jolted me out of my thoughts. She was looking at me expectantly, obviously ready to go.

I hugged my sister again, and Harlow and I were out the door.

"You have such a great family," she said as we walked toward the SUV.

"Yeah, what about Cooper?"

"He's a little...intense," Harlow replied. "But he was really nice to me. I can tell he's incredibly smart, just like the rest of you."

"He's smarter," I confessed. "He's always registered a higher IQ score than Riley, Hudson, or me."

"Is that painful?" she teased.

"Only when I try to beat him at chess," I quipped. "I gave up."

She was quiet for a few seconds before she said, "Taylor asked me to be her maid of honor."

"I hope you agreed. I told Hudson I'd be his best man. Not that anyone would know it, but I think Cooper was touched when Taylor asked him to walk her down the aisle."

"Of course I agreed," she said. "Nobody deserves a happily-ever-after more than Taylor."

"What about you?" I asked curiously.

After putting her purse and her jacket on the hood, she turned toward me and leaned against the SUV like she was in no hurry to get in. "I think you were right when you said that I should give myself some short-term rewards. I'd like to do that once in a while, and live a little more in the moment. I'm way too regimented, and too much of a planner. I'll never change that, and I'm not sure if I want to, but I think I can relax a little. I nearly died, and it's kind of sad that I can't think of one fun, indulgent, or impulsive thing I've done for well over a year."

"Sounds like a plan. Anything I can do to help?"

"Maybe," she said in a slightly flirty voice I'd never heard before.

"Whatever you want, Harlow. Name it and it's yours," I told her as I moved a little closer. Hell, there was nothing I wouldn't do to keep her smiling and happy just like this.

She laughed. "I don't want things. Maybe just a few favors. You know I'm not going to really need an advisor much longer, right?"

"Yeah," I said in a husky voice. "I've been thinking about that, too, but I'm not planning on going anywhere."

"That's good. I don't want you to go anywhere."

I let out a relieved breath. I'd been preparing myself for her to tell me she was good without an advisor, and that it wasn't really necessary for us to get together all that often anymore.

"Okay, so I'd love it if you'd let me drive your Bugatti," she said hesitantly. "We could go someplace where there's no traffic—outside of the city. You could help me so I don't scratch it or something, but I think I'd like to see what it's like to pilot that rocket just once."

Okay, so *that* was definitely not something I'd expected to hear.

I grinned like an idiot as I saw the hopeful look in her eyes. "Sweetheart, you can drive any one of my vehicles any time you want. They're just cars. Although I guarantee that once you feel that kind of power, you'll want to do it again. I have property outside of the city where I run my cars on tracks or straightaways."

"I just want to do it once," she insisted. "I want to try things I've never done before, and have experiences that are new to me. Who knows? I might even drop the cash for one of your must-try, pricier restaurants."

"I was planning on taking you to all of them, Harlow. I just needed to know you were comfortable enough to go," I informed her.

I didn't want Harlow dropping any of her own cash when I could easily take her to every single one of those restaurants.

"No. I'll take you," she insisted. "I have plenty of money in my bank account. It wouldn't be the same if I wasn't laying out the cash. I want to see what it feels like to do something completely frivolous, and I want to do it with you. Maybe it's not much considering everything you've done for me, but I want to do this for you."

I swallowed the lump in my throat as I met Harlow's eyes, and noticed the sincerity in her gaze.

I couldn't remember the last time someone else had insisted on paying for anything when they were with me. So just the fact that Harlow had insisted, and was willing to toss out her hard-earned savings to pay for our dinner, meant a lot to me.

If she was really determined to try one of those restaurants, it would have cost her a lot less to just go by herself.

"Dinner for one is cheaper," I joked.

She shook her head. "I'd never go without you. They're your favorites."

"We'll see," I said vaguely, desperate to change the subject.

Her face fell. "You don't want to go?"

Shit! Now I'd gone and thrown her offer back in her face. The last thing I wanted to do was hurt her.

I was just totally inept at dealing with a woman as sweet as Harlow who wanted to do something for *me*. Just because…she gave a shit about me.

I was used to taking care of *her*, and I was a hell of a lot more comfortable with *that*.

"I do want to go. I'm just not crazy about the idea of you paying, but we'll work it out. Tell me what else you want," I acknowledged hoarsely as I wrapped my fingers around a lock of her hair, and tested the texture.

Huge mistake! It felt like silk and sin, and I gritted my teeth to stop myself from giving in to the temptation to bury both my hands into those beautiful curls.

"I want to tell you something," she said in a sexy whisper.

"Tell me."

"I told you I was attracted to you when you asked me out two years ago, but I never told you that it never went away." She wrapped her arms around my neck. "So if you're still attracted to me, I want you to kiss me just once, so I can see what it feels like."

And...my fucking heart just stopped beating.

I searched her expression, wondering if she was messing with me, but all I saw was a woman who really looked like she wanted me to kiss her.

My heart restarted with an enormous jolt.

If I was still attracted to her?

Christ! Didn't she already know that I wanted to kiss her more than I wanted to suck in my next breath?

Just once, my ass.

If I got one taste of Harlow, I was going to be well and truly fucked.

She started to drop her arms as she said, "I'm sorry. I shouldn't have asked for that. Attractions do go away, and—"

I grasped her wrists as I growled, "Don't!"

I pulled her arms around my neck again, and gave in to the temptation to bury my hands into her hair. "This is going to happen a hell of a lot more than once, sweetheart," I warned her before I tilted her head up, and lowered my mouth to hers.

My plan was to make this first kiss a sweet, tender embrace, something that Harlow might always remember as romantic.

Those plans went completely off the rails when she let out a low moan against my lips, and tightened her arms around my neck.

After that, there was nothing but the rampant desire flowing between the two of us, and the need to get as close as we could get.

She threaded her hands into my hair, and I relished the feel of her nails against my scalp.

I realized the two of us were literally devouring each other outside, in my brother's driveway, but Harlow was so damn sweet I couldn't seem to stop.

I am not going to fuck her on the hood of my damn vehicle like a horny teenager!

Harlow deserved a hell of a lot better than that shit.

I finally tore my mouth from hers, and both of us came up panting.

Harlow looked stunned when she finally opened her eyes.

"Jax," she whispered. "What in the hell just happened?"

"We just found out what it would feel like if we kissed," I told her tightly. "And it was fucking mind-blowing."

I leaned down to give her a more affectionate, sweeter kiss…until I was distracted by a quick flash of light.

And then another.

And another.

"Mr. Montgomery, is this one of your one-date women?"

"Who is she, Mr. Montgomery?"

"Son of a bitch! It's the goddamn press!" I told Harlow as I shielded her with my body.

A large hand clapped my shoulder as I heard Cooper's voice. "Seth said the local press has been hanging around here lately. He left the gate open so we could get out, and the assholes invited themselves in. I'll buy you some time. Get the hell out of here."

"Harlow, get in the car," I instructed as I pulled her body against me.

She snagged her jacket and her purse before I led her to the passenger door and got her inside. I'd tried to shield her the best I could, but the damn picture-taking never stopped.

Neither did the questions that I didn't even acknowledge.

I learned a long time ago that it was best to say nothing when the media found me with a woman. No matter what I said, it would end up misconstrued.

As soon as I put the vehicle in gear, I could hear Seth outside, warning the trespassers that he'd already called the police.

As we exited the driveway, Harlow asked, "What is Cooper doing?"

A quick glance at my brother told me exactly what he was doing. Cooper was definitely buying us a lot of time.

"He's letting all of the air out of the tires of their media van," I said with a smile. "I'm going to owe him one for this."

Harlow

"I don't want to argue with you about this, Harlow. Just pack up some of your stuff so we can get out of here," Jax said gruffly as he waved his hand toward the bedroom of my apartment.

I huffed. "I'm not going to let a bunch of rude reporters chase me out of my own apartment. They were Citrus Beach reporters. It was a small, local channel."

"Yeah, and those stories travel fast. How long do you think it will take before you're identified, and every channel in Southern California is outside your door? You need to be somewhere secure right now unless you really *want* the media looking into your windows, and beating down your door. You won't get a moment of peace, Harlow," Jax rumbled irritably.

I folded my arms over my chest. "Would it really be that bad?"

"You have no fucking idea. There's only one way in, and one way out of this place. You're in a ground-floor apartment," he growled. "You'd be apartment bound again, and this time, it *would* be my fault. My place is secure. Nobody is getting past the gate. Honestly,

I'm not even sure they'd come to Coronado, but they'd hunt you down here just to try to get a story out of you."

Just the thought of being stuck in my tiny apartment with media blocking my only way out had me scurrying toward the bedroom.

I yanked a suitcase out of my closet, and started piling some clothing into it.

Jax knew a lot more about this crazy media stuff than I did, so I trusted his judgment. There was no point in arguing with him. "It annoys the hell out of me that I could feel intimidated in my own home," I told Jax as I started tossing underwear into my bag.

"I know. I'm sorry," he answered as he leaned against the doorjamb of the bedroom with his hands in his pockets. "Don't panic. We have time."

"I'm not *panicked*," I explained. "I'm *pissed*. First, those assholes interrupt the hottest kiss I've ever experienced in my life. Then, I have to worry about them coming after me like hounds after a rabbit to get a damn story. I'm trusting you on this one, but part of me wants to stay just so I can sit here and roll stink bombs out the door. Or figure out some way to mess with their heads. Nobody should be cornered that way for doing nothing more than kissing a smoking-hot guy."

Jax chuckled. "Stink bombs?"

I sent him an admonishing glare. "Obviously, firecrackers are out since they could actually hurt someone, but some really good stink bombs would get them to scatter in a hurry."

"Have I ever mentioned how gorgeous you are when you're pissed off?" Jax asked huskily.

"You've never really seen me angry," I reminded him.

"I haven't," he admitted. "But now that I have, it's incredibly sexy."

I let out an exasperated breath as I looked at the grin on his face, and pointed my finger at him. "Don't shoot me that sexy, panty-melting smile because you think it's going to calm me down. It's your hotness that got me into this position in the first place."

His grin grew broader. "You did ask me to kiss you," he reminded me hoarsely.

I went into the small bathroom to gather my toiletries. "I asked you to *kiss* me," I said in a louder voice so he could hear me. "I didn't ask you to curl my toes and turn the entire universe upside down."

That kiss hadn't been just a simple kiss. It had been like having an orgasmic experience with my clothes on.

I'd been ready to climb up that hard body of his and demand that he fuck me immediately.

I slammed my toiletries bag closed and zipped it before I walked back to my suitcase and shoved it inside.

"Are you really mad because you enjoyed it?" Jax asked in a sensual, low baritone that sent a tingle down my spine, and landed directly between my thighs.

"Yes! No! God, I don't know," I said with a low moan. "I completely lost control. I didn't even notice that the damn press was right on top of us."

I always did things in a measured, cautious sort of way.

I paid attention to details.

I took a deep breath and let it out. "I shouldn't have asked you to kiss me. I did one impulsive thing in my entire life, and it ended up being caught on camera. It would probably be a lot safer if I just stuck to my boring old life."

"But not nearly as much fun," Jax answered provocatively. "Everything will be fine, Harlow. It won't be long before the press gets bored and moves on to another story. They always do. I just want you to stay with me so I know you're safe. I don't want you to feel like you're in a fishbowl being watched all the time."

"Why does it just feel like I'm running from a bunch of bullies?" I asked him in a calmer voice. "I hate that. It's not like I committed a damn crime."

"Then pretend that you're just coming to my place because you want to, and because I invited you to come hang out with me. I know it feels really intrusive, but in this situation, it's just better to remove yourself from it for the sake of your sanity. Most of the gossip and entertainment press aren't dangerous, but they're relentless and annoying. Why deal with that if you don't have to?" he asked.

I nodded. "You're right. It's not a battle I'm going to win. I think I'm about ready."

The press had been chasing celebrities for stories for a long time. If there was nothing I could do to stop it, I might as well be as comfortable as possible.

Jax moved forward until I could feel his hard body against my back. "Look at me, sweetheart," he rumbled.

I turned, looked up, and fell into his gorgeous green-eyed gaze.

"Are you okay?" he asked in a concerned tone.

He was doing it again.

Checking in.

Gauging where my emotions were with a single look.

"I'm okay," I told him honestly.

"You sure?" he asked as he scrutinized my face.

And…my heart melted.

The most difficult Jax to resist was *this one*, the guy who cared about how I was feeling, and wasn't afraid to show his concern.

"I think I was just mad because I let them catch me off guard like that. It was slightly mortifying," I told him honestly. "And I really do hate running away."

"Unfortunately, this shit is part of my world," he said, his voice dripping with regret.

My heart ached because I could see how much he hated exposing me to anything that might upset me.

And I hated the guilt I could see all over his face.

He was right. This *was* part of his world. Maybe they did chase Jax more than his brothers, but Taylor had recently been hounded by the press, too. Once word had gotten out that Hudson might have to be removed from the world's richest, most eligible bachelor list, everyone wanted to know who had captured him.

If I wanted to be part of Jax's world in any way, even as a friend, the media interest was something I was going to have to learn to brush off.

If I had to choose between not having Jax in my life at all, *or* being with him with the media in my face, I'd learn to handle the press.

I lifted my hand and stroked his tight jaw. "Hey, none of this is your fault. I was just venting my frustration," I told him calmly. "It is part of your world, and it's nothing I can't handle. I just need to find a place that sells good stink bombs in quantity. You don't have to protect me anymore, Jax. And for God's sake, don't feel guilty about who you are. You're a billionaire Montgomery. People are always going to be curious about you and your family. There's nothing you can do about that."

He stroked a hand through my hair as he said gruffly, "You never wanted this kind of attention."

"Maybe not," I admitted. "But I'm perfectly willing to put up with it if that means I can hang out with you."

His expression was hopeful as he asked, "Are you? Because I swear I'll hurt those assholes if they scare you away."

I wrapped my arms around his neck and smiled. "I'm a whole lot tougher than you think."

Really, I couldn't blame Jax for thinking that I was fragile. All he'd done was spend time with me during the most vulnerable period of my life. I'd been leaning on him for support, and he'd given it freely, patiently, and generously. But I was ready for the dynamics of this whole relationship to change.

Jax needed to know that he had my support, and that I cared about him, too.

He wrapped his arms around my waist. "You're getting pretty damn feisty," he teased.

"Do you have a problem with that?" I asked.

"Oh, hell no, sweetheart," he rasped. "It nearly killed me to see you like you were on day one. I'd rather have you fight with me than to see you give up on the entire world. If I never have to see you that upset and unhappy, it would be too damn soon. All I want to do is make you happy, Harlow. Just tell me how to do it, and I'll make damn sure you're smiling every day."

Tears sprang to my eyes as I looked at the fierce expression on his face.

He was dead serious, and at that moment, I realized that Jax Montgomery really would do anything just to make me smile.

"You already make me happy," I told him as my heart started to race out of control. "You don't have to do anything else. You're the reason I'm smiling now. You're the reason I'm recovering, and standing on my own two feet now. You have no idea how grateful I am for that."

His expression was intense as he growled, "I don't want you to be grateful. I want you to be happy."

"Then kiss me," I whispered. "Just kiss me."

"I can do that," he grumbled as he lowered his mouth to mine.

If I'd thought that the first kiss was never going to be duplicated, or that it had just been a product of my sexual frustration, I'd been thinking like a fool.

Jax overwhelmed my senses from the second his lips touched mine, and I was completely lost all over again.

My world tilted as he devoured my mouth, consuming *it* and *me* until I was desperate to feel more of him, touch more of him.

Liquid heat flooded between my thighs. I moaned against his lips, and leaned into him until we couldn't get any closer with our clothes on.

A need I'd never experienced before clawed at me, and I speared my hands into his coarse hair, and held on for dear life.

I'd never felt as alive as I did when Jax was touching me like this, and I relished his fierceness, and the way he couldn't seem to get enough of me, either.

He stroked his hand down my back, cupped my ass, and pulled my hips up against him until I could feel exactly how much he wanted me.

And it made me completely insane.

Just knowing I could make his cock that damn hard was a heady feeling, but I wanted more…

"Jax," I whimpered when he released my mouth and ran his tongue down my neck and then up to my earlobe.

"Christ, Harlow," he rasped against my ear. "You make me fucking crazy. Do you have any idea how much I want you naked right now?"

"Oh, God yes," I moaned. "I need you."

"You have me," he growled.

"Show me," I begged.

"Not. Right. Now." He pulled away from me with a groan. "We have to go, baby. I'm not starting anything I can't finish."

He backed off, and I felt that loss almost immediately.

Our eyes locked, and I shuddered as I saw the raw desire in his possessive gaze.

I wasn't sure how long we stood there like that, just staring into each other's eyes as we caught our breath.

I knew that he wanted me.

He knew that I needed him.

And those emotions drifted through the air around us even though we weren't touching.

My hands were shaking as I finally turned and zipped my suitcase.

Once again, I'd lost complete control.

If Jax hadn't found the strength to break away from that craziness, I probably would have torn his clothes off by now.

I shook my head. "You're right. We really have to go."

I probably never should have asked for that kiss, but the temptation to feel those sinful lips on mine had been too damn overwhelming.

Jax lifted my suitcase, and I led him out of the bedroom.

We exited the apartment and I was locking the door when Jax said in a guttural voice, "I want you to know that was one of the hardest damn things I've ever done."

I tried to hide a small smile as I finished locking up.

Considering that Jax Montgomery had probably been to hell and back many times between the SEALs and Last Hope, that was one hell of a statement.

Chapter 16

Jax

"How's Harlow doing?" Hudson asked. "If I'd known the press were crawling around Seth and Riley's place, I never would have left."

I leaned back in the chair in my home office, trying not to think about the fact that Harlow was upstairs and naked in the guest suite bathtub.

I was trying to back off a little so Harlow could wind down.

The last thing she'd needed was the press drama tonight when she was still trying to find normal again.

"She's actually handled it pretty well," I told him. "I think she's more pissed off than she is anxious. I guess since this has always been part of our lives, I have to remember it's all new to her."

"Yeah," Hudson agreed. "Taylor had pretty much the same reaction when we were cornered in a restaurant. She doesn't back down easily, either."

"I'd rather see Harlow pissed than upset," I said. "Hopefully, she'll learn to ignore them as much as possible, eventually."

"You say that like she's going to be around for a while," Hudson said thoughtfully. "So what the hell is the deal with you two?"

Now that I had the chance, I told Hudson everything.

He asked a few questions, but mostly he just listened to me spill my guts.

"Why in the hell didn't you tell me?" Hudson grumbled.

"Harlow asked me not to tell you because she didn't want Taylor to know that she was struggling," I explained. "She figured Taylor had enough on her plate, and she didn't want her to worry. She wanted to get her head together first."

"Taylor was worried about her," Hudson said. "I think she had her suspicions that something wasn't right, but she wanted to give Harlow her space to grieve Mark. Taylor said that she and Harlow had worked everything out by the time we crashed their party on the patio."

Harlow hadn't told me that, but then, she really hadn't had a chance. "I'm glad. I think it was important for the two of them to really talk so Harlow could finish healing. She was carrying a lot of guilt, and I knew talking to Taylor would help."

"Judging by the way Harlow looked earlier, I would imagine that she won't need your advisor services much longer," Hudson said contemplatively.

"Doesn't matter," I said defensively. "We'll still be together. I'd prefer it wasn't an advisor/victim relationship anyway."

"Friends?" Hudson asked curiously.

"If I have to stay strictly in the friend zone with her for another fucking day, I'll lose my mind," I said grumpily. "I've been in that role for almost a month. It wasn't difficult when Harlow was really vulnerable. She needed me to be her friend. Now that she's stronger, and is on the road to taking her life back, it's pure hell. I'm attracted to her, Hudson. And I'm not talking about a mild attraction. Harlow gets to me and makes me completely insane. It's probably way too soon to ask her for anything more, but if I don't, I'll lose it. She feels the same way I do, which makes keeping my hands off her an impossibility. I was kissing her for the first time when the damn media interrupted. Fuck! I want to do what's right for her, but I don't see the two of us getting this shit under control. I'm going to try to back off to give her more time, but I'm not sure how long it will last."

"She's staying with you now, right?" Hudson questioned.

"Yeah."

"You're screwed," Hudson informed me. "I think you need to let her decide when and if she's ready to change the relationship. Maybe it seems too soon to you, but it's possible that she might not feel the same way. It sounds like she's accepted Mark's death, and the fact that the two of them may not have worked out in a romantic sense. Is this just a physical thing?"

"No," I said honestly. "It would probably be easier if it was, but that's just part of it. I've always had this strange connection to Harlow. I was actually pretty disappointed when she turned me down two years ago. I won't say that I didn't date after that, but I pretty much lost any real interest in seeing anyone else. Since the kidnapping, I've stopped dating altogether. I was obsessed about getting Harlow to talk to me, even when I didn't know how bad things were for her."

"Yeah," Hudson said solemnly. "I noticed that you'd slowed down on the dating, but I wasn't quite sure why. What happened to the brother who used to tell me that loving someone was a choice?"

Love? Am I in love with Harlow?

I didn't have to ask myself that question again. I knew the answer.

"Christ! Those words are coming back to haunt me," I said. "I can't turn off the way I feel about Harlow, and I can't choose not to feel this way. I was a dumbass when I said that."

"Not really," Hudson defended. "It's not like we had very good examples of what a great relationship was like when we were younger. I was totally unprepared when I met Taylor. How in the hell were we supposed to know that meeting the right woman would turn our whole world upside down?"

"I didn't," I said flatly. "I can't fuck this up, Hudson, but I don't know how to deal with a woman who really gives a damn about *me*. Harlow isn't impressed by the Montgomery name, or the fact that I'm a billionaire who could give her every damn material thing her heart desires. She sees me, and honestly, as much as I've always wanted that to happen, now that it has, it scares the shit out of me. I'm not used to a woman who wants more than just expensive gifts or to be seen with an ultra-wealthy Montgomery. Hell, Harlow wants to take *me* to dinner and let *her* pay for it. I didn't even know how to respond to something like that. Things just don't work that way in our world."

Hudson chuckled. "Get used to it. Harlow has been independent her entire adult life. It's her way of showing you that she cares about you. When Taylor does something thoughtful for me, it throws me for a loop, too. I'm pretty damn grateful every damn time she does something for me just because she cares, but it's just completely foreign to me. So, I get it. We want that, but it's not something we ever really thought would happen. I guess we don't really feel worthy sometimes, but I'm starting to shake that shit off. I want Taylor to love me like that, and she shows me every single day that *she* thinks I deserve it. After a while, I started to believe her. I'm not sure how I ended up with a woman like Taylor, but there's never going to be a day that I'm not profoundly grateful that she loves me. The only way you'll screw this up is if you can't learn to accept the way that Harlow cares, and you throw it back in her face. Maybe one of the hardest things to acknowledge is that when a woman cares about you that way, you have the power to hurt her."

I thought about the way I'd reacted to Harlow when she'd offered to take me out to dinner, and I felt like a complete asshole all over again. "Yeah, I already kind of screwed up. Harlow put herself out there, and I backed off because I didn't know how to handle it."

"Take my advice—don't do that shit," Hudson advised. "Be honest and tell her how you feel. Things can go south in a hurry if you don't communicate. You'll have to decide which is more important to you—being loved by Harlow, or not putting yourself out there, too, and never taking a risk. With a woman like her, you can't have both."

"I have no idea if she loves me or not. It's just been a friendship until today."

Hudson released an audible breath. "I used to think I couldn't have it both ways with Taylor, but I was wrong. She's my best friend, and I wouldn't have it any other way. She knows all of my strengths and my weaknesses, and still loves me anyway. The only way you're going to know if Harlow loves you is to put your heart out there, Jax."

"And if she butchers it into tiny little pieces?" I asked morosely.

"I don't think that's going to happen, but if it does, you'll know she isn't the right woman for you," Hudson said philosophically.

"Yeah, I'm sure I'll find that knowledge comforting while I'm laying on the floor bleeding out," I grumbled. "Fuck that! Harlow is going to be mine."

"If that's the case," Hudson mused, "then you'll have to work to make it happen. I know you, Jax. You can charm the hell out of anyone you meet. You've always been a lot better at that than I'll ever be."

"Everyone except *her*," I corrected. "She messes with my head until I don't know what to say, and she doesn't fall for any of my usual bullshit. She never has."

"Good," Hudson replied smugly. "You need someone who can see right through that and throw you off your game."

I raked a frustrated hand through my hair. "I love her, Hudson. I think I probably have since the first day we met. Just the thought of losing her makes me come completely unglued."

"Then don't lose her," he suggested. "Make her happy. You said Seth and Mason were crazy because they'd probably move mountains just to make Riley and Laura happy. Have you changed your mind about that?"

"I take back every single thing I said about them and you," I said gruffly. "Hell, maybe I had to convince myself that falling in love was a choice because Harlow had already turned me down flat. It killed me that first day I saw her after the kidnapping. She seemed so damn defeated, and there's nothing I wouldn't do to never have to see her like that again. I still wish I'd gone to see her in person way before I did. All I had to do was take one look at her, and I knew something wasn't right. She looked like she'd been battling demons, and was on the losing side of that fight. She's so damn stubborn that she thought she could fix everything herself."

"It's not easy reaching out for help when you've never had to do it before," Hudson considered. "She's obviously tough. Harlow did six years active duty Air Force, and apparently thrived. Anyone who can juggle working full-time while they're pursuing a doctorate has to have the kind of determination that most people don't. She might be hardheaded, but she's had to be to get to where she is today. I say that when she's ready, she'd be an amazing asset to Last Hope if that's still what she wants."

"I think she's even more determined to do it now than she was at the beginning. She has a big heart. She'd already have all the equipment up and running if she had her way."

Hudson chuckled. "Maybe you should let her have her way. Do you think she'll come back to Montgomery?"

"Most likely," I answered. "She hasn't mentioned that yet, but I think she's getting stir-crazy. I just don't want her to rush the rest of her recovery, and she will if she thinks she can get away with it."

"I think she should take some time to take care of herself," Hudson agreed. "She doesn't have to rush. Her position will be waiting for her when she's ready."

"I'd like to be around to make sure she does," I said. "I want to take some time off, Hudson. I'd like to spend some time with Harlow as something other than her advisor."

"You and Cooper covered my ass when I needed time," Hudson replied. "Is there any question that I'd do the same for you? It's been a long time since you had any real time away from Montgomery. Take all the time you need. We worked our asses off to get our company to where it is now. We don't really need to work that hard anymore. That's why we have all our top-level executives."

I snorted. "Yeah, we saw how well that went while we were all away at Mason's wedding."

It had been our top-level executives who had screwed up the entire kidnapping situation in the first place.

"We cleaned house," Hudson reminded me. "I think we have better people in those positions now. Besides, it's not like we have to test them out now. Cooper and I will be there."

"Thanks," I said sincerely.

"Keep in touch and let me know how things are going," he instructed. "Now that Harlow is doing better, have some fun."

"She wants to drive my Chiron," I told him with a smile on my face. "I might have to take her out to the tracks. I'm pretty sure there's a secret adrenaline junkie underneath that organized and rational exterior of hers."

"And you're actually going to let her drive it?" Hudson asked in a surprised tone. "That's a hell of a lot of horsepower for a female with no experience driving something like the Bugatti."

"She'll be with me," I told him. "I'm not about to see her get hurt, and I think she can handle it."

"I'm sure she can," Hudson agreed.

"She hasn't asked me for much of anything, so I wasn't about to tell her *no*. Harlow is trying to spread her wings, and I'm more than happy to help her fly."

As a matter of fact, I was making it my personal mission to find so many new and different experiences for Harlow that I could watch her soar like an eagle.

Nothing in this world could make me happier than that.

Chapter 17

Harlow

"I think you're completely insane, Jax Montgomery. Who rents out an entire Michelin-star restaurant just to avoid being bothered by the press!"

There was no sting in my words, and Jax just grinned back at me as he enjoyed a glass of seventy-five-year-old cognac.

It wasn't the first time in the last week that I'd wondered if Jax had gone completely mad, and I doubted it would be the last.

My eyes roamed over him. We'd dressed up for this occasion. I was wearing a black cocktail dress, and Jax was deliciously handsome in one of his custom suits.

I leaned back in my chair and took a sip of my wine. We'd been in the restaurant for hours, savoring each new course as it came to our table.

Luckily, the portions had been small, or someone would have had to roll me out of this beautiful restaurant on a cart.

"It's your birthday, Harlow, and it wasn't that big of a deal," he remarked as he swirled his cognac around in the glass. "Did you enjoy it?"

"You know I did," I scolded. "But you're spoiling me shamelessly."

"No, I'm not, but you nixed all my other birthday ideas," he reminded me.

"Because every one of them included your private jet and an international destination," I told him.

It wasn't like I didn't want to fly in his private jet, and escape to a tropical location, but my passport had just expired. It also would have been a very extreme gift for a birthday.

"I told you we could switch it to something in the US, Hawaii or Florida. We'll get your passport renewed soon."

"I think this is quite enough, thank you. It's been an amazing birthday for me," I said happily. "It was good to have a day without some kind of extreme adventure. I've loved every single one of them, but it's nice to just be with you like this."

We'd driven to Carlsbad earlier in the day so I could spend some time with Mom on my birthday. It was no surprise that she'd ended up hugging Jax like a long-lost son before the day was over.

Jax had a way of endearing himself to people by listening to them like he really gave a damn about what they were telling him. He found a way to connect with almost everyone he met.

He'd ended up bonding with my mother over mystery novels and cupcake flavors, two things that were near and dear to my mother's heart.

I'd never known that Jax was so well-versed on those two subjects, but I really shouldn't be surprised. He had a voracious appetite for knowledge on almost any subject, and he seemed to suck it up and retain it like a sponge.

The photo that had been taken of me and Jax hadn't been completely scandalous, but the article had torn him to shreds...again. The media had gone from camping outside my apartment to Jax's doorstep on Coronado Island. Luckily, Jax's place was so secure that we barely even noticed them, unless we were going out and we saw the reporters as we drove through the front gate.

We'd been outside almost every single day since I'd gotten to Jax's house a week ago.

I'd driven his Chiron, and it had been exhilarating. I'd never driven anything that moved that fast in my entire life, and I hadn't even gotten close to maximum speed.

I'd also done a tandem skydive with Jax. I'd had to push myself to make *that* leap, but since Jax was qualified to do tandems, and I'd been doubling with him, it hadn't felt completely terrifying.

We'd experienced a private parasailing trip, too, but that hadn't been as frightening as jumping out of a plane.

We'd been on the go every day, nonstop. Jax had sought out so many new adventures for me in the last week that my head had never stopped spinning.

The only thing he *hadn't* done was try to get me naked and sweaty. Oh, he was affectionate, and I couldn't even count the number of mind-blowing kisses he'd laid on me over the last week. However, he never let things go too far.

Is he afraid of pushing me too fast?

If he was, he was giving me way too much time.

At this point, I was beyond primed, and completely ready to go. I had been since the first time he'd kissed me.

"Happy birthday, sweetheart," Jax said huskily as he handed me an elaborately wrapped gift.

I picked up the present from the table with surprise. "Jax, you've given me an outrageous amount of gifts today already."

He'd had a pile of gifts waiting for me at the breakfast table. Those packages had contained everything from a new laptop computer, which I had really needed, to a gorgeous pair of white gold and diamond earrings.

The earrings were beautiful, and I was wearing them tonight, but they'd been a hard present to accept. I'd recognized the quality of those diamonds. I'd shuddered over the possible price tag. And then I'd reminded myself that *Jax* didn't see the gift as extravagant at all, and the last thing I wanted to do was reject a gift so thoughtfully given. It was obvious he'd chosen them himself because they were exactly my style. So, I'd thanked him with tears in my eyes, and a kiss.

There wasn't much else I could have done in that situation.

Jax was, in fact, a billionaire, and *his* normal and *my* normal were two different things.

What seemed like a crazy expensive gift to me wasn't pricey to him, and really, all he'd wanted to do was please me.

His thoughtfulness had touched me more than the actual gift.

However, I was really hoping I'd have time to get used to his life-style before he presented me with another insanely expensive gift.

I pulled off the giftwrap, and exposed a red box about the size of my hand.

After I lifted the lid, I pulled out the necklace inside.

"It's not an expensive gift," Jax explained. "There's a story behind it."

The diamond-cut, white gold chain hadn't come cheap, but as I fingered the pendant, I knew he was telling the truth.

It was a four-leaf clover, encased in acrylic to preserve it.

"Tell me the story." I was intrigued, and eager to hear it.

"The pendant used to belong to a buddy of mine in the Navy. I replaced the black cord with a more feminine chain for you, but I wore that clover on every single date I've been on since I got out of the military. Jeremy said he found it in a field right before he went into the Navy, and wore it until he found the love of his life. He gave it to me, and made me promise I'd wear it when I went out with somebody new. He swore it would eventually lead me to the right woman."

I kept stroking my thumb over the pendant as I said, "He was obviously happy with how it worked for him."

Jax nodded. "His marriage was one of the few happy ones. He was crazy about his wife, and she loved him enough that she tolerated all of the bad parts of being married to a SEAL."

"Do you think it worked for you?" I asked.

His expression was thoughtful as he said, "I used to think it didn't. Obviously, none of my dates ever led me to the right woman, but now I'm beginning to wonder if it just worked in a different way. Maybe it weeded out all the wrong ones until I found you, Harlow.

I want you to have that because my one-off dating days are over. I'll never need that again as long as you're with me."

My heart was racing as our gazes locked. "What will you tell your Navy buddy?"

"Nothing. He was killed in the line of duty a few weeks after he gave that to me, but I'd like to think he'd be happy that I don't have to wear that four-leaf clover anymore," Jax said hoarsely.

I wrapped my hand around the whole necklace, and clutched it as tears marched down my face. "I'm so sorry, Jax."

"Don't cry, sweetheart," Jax said with a frown. "I grieved for Jeremy a long time ago. That four-leaf clover was a good memory, which is why I always wore it like he asked me to do. Now that I don't need it anymore, I thought you might like to have it."

I knew exactly what he was doing, which was why I couldn't stop crying. He was giving me something that meant something to him. Jax was also trying to let me know that he was serious about this relationship, and that his dating days were over.

The necklace had a long enough chain that I was able to slip it over my head. After I did, I wrapped my fingers around the pendant again. "This is the sweetest gift anyone has ever given me," I told him earnestly. "I'll keep it safe."

It wasn't just a gift; it was a promise that warmed my heart.

He shook his head. "You don't really have to wear it."

"Oh, yes, I do," I told him adamantly.

Not only had it belonged to Jax, but it had also been in possession of someone he'd cared about. I wasn't *ever* taking it off.

"I have one more surprise for you," he informed me. "But it isn't a physical gift. I want to show you something."

I breathed a sigh of relief that he was done making me cry for the day. "Tell me."

He shook his head. "Nope. I have to *show* you. Have a little patience, woman."

"How am I supposed to be patient when you're keeping it a mystery?" I asked.

"Your mom loves mysteries," he pointed out.

"I'm more of a short story kind of woman," I teased. "I can get right to the story and see how it ends within an hour or two."

"What happens when you want a longer book?" he questioned.

"I read the ending first so it doesn't drive me crazy," I lied.

He lifted a brow, and I burst out laughing. "You don't really do that," he accused.

"I don't," I confessed. "But I can't tell you how many times I've been tempted."

He grinned. "I'm ready whenever you are."

I hopped out of my chair and grabbed my purse.

Jax wrapped his arm around my waist and lifted a hand in goodbye to all the staff.

Since they were all smiling broadly and waving back, I had to assume he'd already paid, and he'd been a very generous tipper.

The valet had Jax's Mercedes SUV ready at the door.

Jax slipped the guy a tip, and waved him off so he could open the passenger door himself.

I turned to him before I got in. "Honestly, this has been the most incredible birthday I've ever had, Jax. It's actually been the most amazing week I've ever had, too. Every single experience was a once-in-a-lifetime thing for me, but the very best part has been spending this time with you. Having you all to myself like this is special to me."

Jax had taken some time off, and he'd spent every possible moment with me.

When I was in counseling in the morning, he was usually planning our adventure for the day.

"You don't think I'm enjoying every moment that I'm with you?" he asked with a grin. "I've walked around for the last week feeling like the luckiest bastard in the world."

My heart skipped a beat as I saw the adoring look in his eyes.

Strange as it might seem to me, I knew he was sincere.

"You're an amazing man, Jax Montgomery," I whispered right before I gave in to the urge to kiss him.

His arm tightened around me, and I could feel the controlled strength of his grip as he kissed me until I was breathless.

"Get in," he said hoarsely as he let me go.

His beautiful eyes were turbulent as he nodded his head toward the passenger seat.

I could sense his barely leashed control starting to crumble, so I slid into the seat and fastened my seat belt.

Jax hopped in and started the SUV. "Are you ready to make that stop before we head back to Coronado?"

"If there's something you want to show me, I'm definitely up for it."

I was game for anywhere he wanted to go right now.

But I'd already decided that once we got back to Coronado, Jax Montgomery was going to be all mine.

I didn't want to spend another night in his guest suite alone.

It was getting torturous for both of us.

If Jax wasn't going to make a move, I was going to end up seducing the hottest man on the planet tonight.

Chapter 18

Harlow

"Jax, where exactly are we?" I asked as he pulled into the parking lot of what looked like a small condo building. "We're pretty close to Montgomery Headquarters."

"We are," he affirmed as he turned off the SUV.

I hopped out of the vehicle and looked at the brick building. It was an unassuming three-story structure, and judging by the amount of windows, it probably didn't house all that many condos.

Jax took my hand and led me to what I assumed was a lobby door. "There's no lights on inside," I said in a hushed voice. "What if everyone is asleep?"

He grinned as he put his finger to a print scanner. "I guarantee that nobody is asleep in this building."

I frowned at him. "How do you know that?"

The lock clicked and he pushed the door open as he said, "Because I own the whole building, sweetheart." He grabbed my hand and pulled me inside. "Welcome to Last Hope Headquarters."

I blinked as the space was flooded with light. There was a small lounge area, but the inside was nothing like I expected it to be.

It took me a few minutes to realize that the exterior was nothing more than a façade. Although the windows probably did have the closed plantation shutters I'd seen from outside, they were blocked from the inside with what looked like heavy-duty, metal security shutters.

"What happens if you need to get out the window?" I asked in an awed tone.

Jax flipped a switch near the door, and all of the shutters lifted. "They can be opened manually, too, but they're pretty heavy." He hit the switch to let them back down.

Obviously, the security in this place was amazing. And it was ingenious to camouflage the whole operations building to make it look like a small, boring condo building.

I suspected it *had* been a condo building at one time, but the interior had been completely overhauled.

I left the small lounge area and wandered into a huge open space that took up the rest of the ground floor.

"The biggest of our operations areas," Jax explained from behind me. "As you can see, Marshall started to set up the weather analysis equipment, but didn't get all the way there."

There were several different stations, and all of them contained tables of what looked like high-tech equipment, computers, and desk chairs.

"This is one hell of a setup for a volunteer organization," I said with amazement.

"We have more operations rooms on the second floor, but this is where we do most of the work," he shared.

I strolled around to the different stations, recognizing some of the GPS and radar equipment, but some of the gadgets were completely foreign. What I didn't recognize, I was sure Jax would explain to me.

When I got to the weather station, I stopped and started sorting through equipment. "This must have cost a small fortune," I said to Jax. "It's top of the line." I crouched and then started crawling for some of the stored boxes underneath.

Jax grabbed the back of my dress and pulled me. "You don't need to do this right now, baby. I just wanted to show you the headquarters. You're not exactly dressed for crawling on the floor, and I'll get everything out for you."

I dusted my hands off. "It won't take me too long to set everything up. I take it Marshall is making me an official volunteer?"

"Yes. Let me just say it's a relief to know you can handle that part of our data."

I squealed and threw myself into his arms. "Thank you! Thank you! Thank you!"

I was so ecstatic I started to kiss every inch of his face.

He wrapped his arms around my waist to steady me. "Damn, woman. I think you're more excited about this than any of your other gifts. It's not that exciting. It's a lot of work for zero pay."

I tightened my arms around his neck as I pulled back and our eyes met. "I'll be part of something important, Jax, so it's worth it to me. I want to help. I'd really like to take my position back at Montgomery, too."

"When you're ready, that job is waiting. I don't want you to rush it."

I stepped back and seated my ass on the table.

Jax sat down in one of the chairs next to me. "So what do you want to know? I'll take you to the other floors and show you around in a few. The third floor really is condos. Hudson, Cooper, and I all have one upstairs in case we need to stay in the city."

"So that's your condo within walking distance of Montgomery."

"Yeah. Like I said, I don't use it much anymore," he replied.

"How in the hell does Marshall manage all this on his own?" I asked. "I know you don't have rescues happening all the time, but when shit hits the fan, how does he collect data from everywhere?"

Jax shrugged. "We all pitch in. If we're working, it's busy. I hate to break it to you, but we aren't the only wealthy brothers involved in San Diego. There's plenty of money flowing into Last Hope, but we don't have the people to do some of the tech work we need. I think Marshall will start being a little more open to possibilities after this."

"How has all of this flown under the radar of the government?" I queried.

"It actually doesn't. Not completely. Several of the agencies know we exist, but officially, we don't. We try not to step on their toes. Any rescues or missions we take on have already been marked as impossible for the government. We get fed referrals because there's nothing more they can do, but they'd never admit they sent the information."

"Do you have volunteers all over the country, or just San Diego?"

"We have some scattered all over the world," he answered. "But most of them are in different locations in the US. You'll meet a few who participate in this area, eventually."

"God, it's amazing that so many guys want to help."

He leaned back in his chair and shot me a wry grin. "I think we do it for our own sanity, too. It's hard when you first get out of Special Forces. It's almost like we forget how to function in the civilian world because we're used to everything being so intense all the time."

"So are you trying to say you were bored?" I asked as I lifted a brow.

"We were pretty busy with Montgomery when we were first discharged, but after that, we probably were. Or maybe we just wanted to feel like we were part of something, too," he drawled.

"You are," I assured him. "Last Hope is unique."

"It is now," he agreed. "There used to be another private rescue operation, but they ended up getting out because of an accident, so they don't exist anymore."

"How do you manage to juggle everything, Jax? Your company, Last Hope, the work you do at the dog training center?" It was a lot of responsibility for one man.

"It's not a big deal," he answered nonchalantly. "Rescues only pop up every so often, and I do the dog training when I have time. I have Cooper and Hudson at Montgomery, so it isn't like I'm handling the company alone."

As usual, Jax wasn't going to give himself a single ounce of credit for the things he did. "Someday, you're going to realize that you're pretty extraordinary," I insisted.

"I doubt it," he drawled. "Hell, I'm actually afraid that someday *you'll* figure out that I'm not."

"Never going to happen," I told him softly as I stroked my fingers through his hair.

It was astonishing that a man like Jax could have any insecurities, but Riley had been correct when she'd said his childhood had left a mark that might never go away.

I could feel his hesitation about me sometimes, and I hated it.

Like I was going anywhere without a really good reason to leave?

I was crazy about Jax.

I just wasn't sure if *he* knew that.

"You do realize that our advisor agreement ended a few days ago?" he said in a teasing voice.

"As far as I'm concerned, it ended the first time you kissed me," I said with a laugh. "I don't need an advisor anymore, Jax. I have a good therapist, and we make a little more progress every day. Not that I'm not grateful that you were my advisor, but that's not what I need from you anymore."

"What do you need?" he asked gruffly.

"An equal partnership," I explained. "I had to lean on you pretty heavy for a while, and that was never fair to you."

He shook his head. "I never saw it like that, Harlow. I didn't mind that you needed me."

God, sometimes this man said such sweet things without even knowing he was saying them.

"Maybe I want you to need me, too, Jax," I muttered.

"You have no idea how much I need you, Harlow," he rasped. "You're the first damn woman who's even seen *me*, and not the billionaire mogul with the Montgomery name. Do you really think there's a ton of women out there who give a damn what kind of food I like, or what restaurants are my favorite? Do you think they believe that training dogs for veterans with PTSD is a good way to spend my free time? Hell, you're actually the first woman I've even told about that. Most of the women in my social sphere aren't dog lovers, and I guarantee all of them would be bitching about dog hair on their new designer clothing if I introduced them to Molly or Tango. I don't fit into that world. Maybe I never did. But I grew up in it, so it's what I'm used to. I did the club scene to see what else was out there, but I told you how that turned out. When I met you two years ago, there was something there. I can't explain what the hell it was, but I've never been drawn to a woman like I was to you."

"I felt it, too, Jax," I told him breathlessly. "We...clicked. I never should have blown off that instinct."

"I don't blame you, Harlow. I didn't look like a good risk to you, and I get that. But for fuck's sake, please don't ever think that I don't need you. I've been waiting for you for a long time."

I slid off the table, straddled his lap, and hugged Jax close to me. He locked his arms around me, and rocked me while we clung to each other like we never wanted to be pulled apart.

I wasn't exactly sure how long we stayed like that, but it was quite a while before he got around to finishing his tour of Last Hope Headquarters.

Jax

"**D**o you have any idea what it's like to want a woman until your balls turn blue?" I asked my golden retriever as he watched me pace around my bedroom restlessly. "Nah, you probably don't since you got yours whacked off a long time ago. Sorry, buddy."

Tango tilted his head and looked at me from his position in the middle of my bed. I wasn't sure if he was sympathizing with me, or pissed off because he no longer had balls.

"I can't do this shit anymore," I mumbled, not even sure who I was talking to anymore.

There was nobody in the bedroom except me and Tango.

I'd said those same words every single night, but I'd always managed to get through the following day without getting Harlow naked.

Because every damn morning, I remember that she deserves better.

She wasn't a damn one-nighter, or an occasional screw.

She needed more romance, more fun, more time before I lost my shit and dragged her into my bed like a caveman with absolutely no finesse.

Because…yeah….I already knew that once I really touched her, it was over.

Goodbye, sweet seduction.

Hello, unbridled carnal lust.

So I'd waited, because I'd wanted to be with Harlow, take her on real dates, make her understand that I wanted a lot more than just her body.

Harlow had also been through a hell of a lot, and the last thing I wanted was to push her away by asking for more than she was ready to give.

I'd lasted *seven damn days* with nothing more than a kiss and some very mild groping.

I'd told myself over and over that making her happy was even more important than my need to be burning up the sheets with her every night. And that was no lie.

But once we'd said goodnight, and Harlow headed off to the guest suite? My mind and body went into full-on fantasy mode because I had way too much time to think.

Maybe if I could see some kind of sign that she wants more.

It wasn't like I didn't know that Harlow was attracted to me. It was obvious every time I kissed her.

What in the hell did I want her to do—seduce *me*?

If that was the only thing that was going to convince me that she was ready, I could be waiting for a hell of a long time.

She'd expect me to make that move.

I was Jax Montgomery, celebrated playboy and seducer of women. I was the guy who'd been around the block more than a few times, right?

Honestly, I *had* been with more than my fair share of women, and I hadn't had a second's hesitation about seducing any of them.

I'd also never heard a single complaint once it was over.

Fuck! The problem was that Harlow was different.

She didn't do one-nighters.

It had to be more to her than just…sex.

And I was the guy who could fill her night with multiple orgasms, but I wasn't sure how to give any woman…more. Probably because no women I'd ever been with had ever wanted it. They been just fine with coming until they couldn't do it anymore.

"I just need to get to sleep, and stop obsessing over Harlow Lewis," I grumbled.

I looked at Tango and pointed toward his bed. "Dude, get in your own bed. You know better. You're a bed hog."

Tango was too damn big to crash on my bed, and liked his room to stretch out. He'd commandeer the whole mattress if I let him.

He also snored worse than a full-grown guy.

He shot me a fuck-you look, and hopped off the bed and into his own.

"Good boy," I praised gruffly.

I was just tossing the comforter and sheet back when I heard the bedroom door open. There was one small creak when it opened. It was barely noticeable, but it was audible to me. Probably because I was trained to hear just about any unusual noise.

I jerked my head to look at Tango, and saw that his tail was wagging.

Molly sprinted past me and bounced on top of Tango because she obviously wanted to share his bed.

"Molly, how did you get in here?"

She never left Harlow anymore, even though Harlow hadn't had a nightmare in quite a while. The two of them were bonded.

"My fault. I let her in," Harlow said in a husky voice.

I turned, glad I hadn't shucked my boxer briefs or Harlow would have gotten way more than she'd bargained for by dropping in.

"What's wrong?" I asked, immediately wondering if she'd had another nightmare.

"Nothing," she answered with a shrug.

She was trying to act nonchalant, but her eyes were roaming over me like she'd never seen a half-naked guy before.

I stared back at her, unable to keep my eyes off her scantily clad body.

Okay, the white, halter nightgown she was wearing covered her body down to her ankles, but the silky material was fairly thin. It wasn't overly sexy, but on Harlow, it was completely sensual.

"What do you need, Harlow?" I asked curiously. There weren't many things she didn't know how to find in this house anymore.

She closed the door and leaned against it. "I want you. I'm here to seduce you. I think I've waited long enough for you to make a move, so I'm making one."

Holy fucking fantasies! She couldn't possibly be serious. She looked nervous as hell and ready to bolt.

"You have to be screwing with me," I scoffed.

"No, what I'm saying is that I'd like to be screwing you," she said in a soft voice.

"Come on, Harlow. What do you really need? You're killing me here."

"I'm serious, Jax. I know I'm one of the most boring women on the planet, and I'm not really all that good at this whole seduction thing. Well, actually I've never *really* tried it. I've never been exceptional at flirtation, either. And you know I bombed at the whole club scene. I'm just a science nerd who would really like you to fuck me. God, isn't it past time to get naked and sweaty together? I'm really tired of waiting," she finished with a groan.

My cock was ready to burst the seams of my boxer briefs, but my brain was still trying to figure out what she'd just said.

Had Dr. Harlow Lewis *really* just asked me to fuck her? Holy hell, I knew she wasn't screwing with me. She would have started laughing a long time ago. Right now, she looked vulnerable, and I was fairly certain she really had just offered her body to me.

My heart was slamming against my chest wall as I just stared at her.

I didn't care if she had no experience with being the seducer.

I didn't care if she thought she was boring. Well, except for the fact that it wasn't true.

I didn't care if she wasn't flirty or the kind of woman who could flaunt it in the club scene.

B. A. Scott

Harlow was the sexiest thing I'd ever seen, and she had just sealed her fate by walking into the lion's den.

Maybe she wasn't practiced with seduction, but I had no problem taking it from here.

Harlow is mine!

She was always *supposed* to be mine.

"Oh, God, I'm sorry," she said as she put a hand to her mouth and let out a choked sob. "This isn't something you want at all, is it? Okay, I feel like a total idiot, now. Just forget everything I just said."

She fled the room so fast I wouldn't be surprised if she left tire marks on the hardwood floor.

Shit! I'd just hurt her by not reacting fast enough or saying one damn word about her proposition.

Actually, I'd accused her of screwing with me when she'd been doing something she'd never done before.

How could she possibly *not* know how much I wanted her?

How could she possibly think that I'd ever refuse an offer like the one she just made me?

"Harlow!" I bellowed so loud that both the dogs startled.

Fuck it! I'd find *her.*

We weren't going another night without working this out, and I sure as hell wasn't going to let her cry over this.

I strode out of the master bedroom, closing the door behind me so the dogs would stay in their bed.

I tried to open the door of the guest suite, but the door was locked.

I pounded on it, hard. "Open the damn door, Harlow. We need to talk."

"It can wait until tomorrow," she called in a muffled voice.

Shit! She was *still* crying.

And my fucking heart ached because I knew it.

I folded my arms across my chest. "I'm not leaving until you open this door. I'll camp out here all night. I'll get Tango and Molly to bring snacks if necessary."

"I don't want to talk right now," she called firmly.

Ouch! Okay, that hurt.

There had *never* been a time when Harlow hadn't wanted to talk to me.

We talked about almost every topic imaginable.

I leaned my forehead against the door in frustration. "Don't do this, Harlow. I didn't mean to hurt you. I was just surprised to see you. You didn't even give me a chance to say anything. You're not boring, and that was the hottest seduction attempt I've ever seen. You don't really need to do anything to get my dick hard. All you have to do is stand in front of me and breathe."

"Don't make fun of this," she called in a tearful voice.

"*Christ!* You know me better than that, Harlow. When have I ever done that to you if we were having a serious conversation?"

Something was wrong.

This wasn't like her.

"I just need some time, Jax. We can talk about it tomorrow."

Something told me that giving her time would put more distance between us, but if that's what she needed, I should probably respect her request.

Oh, hell no. I wasn't going to leave her in there, crying alone. She'd dealt with enough fucking unhappiness in the last several months.

I slammed my hand against the door, not quite sure what the hell to do.

Chapter 20

Harlow

I took a deep breath and swiped the tears from my face.

Everything he'd said made perfect sense.

I probably *hadn't* given him a chance to respond, and I shouldn't be punishing *him* for something that wasn't his fault.

He's really not the one who hurt me, and Jax deserves better.

I scrambled off the bed, and rushed to the door, not knowing whether or not Jax had actually given up on talking to me.

I pulled the door open, my heart hammering because I knew I'd made a mistake. I'd jeopardized something really, really good because of my stupid insecurities.

Thankfully, Jax had been a man of his word. He was still right outside the door, waiting for me to let him in, and my heart squeezed painfully as I saw his expression.

He looked forlorn.

He looked frantic.

He looked like a guy who had just been slapped in the face for doing nothing wrong.

"I'm so sorry," I whispered as our eyes met. "This isn't your fault. I know you care about me, and I overreacted. I hurt you, and that's the last thing in the world I'd ever want to do."

"Can I come in?" he asked gruffly. "I think we should talk about this now."

I opened the door, and his expression was unreadable as he entered. *Please don't tell me I've managed to screw up the best thing that's ever happened to me!*

I took a seat on the massive king-size bed, and tucked my legs underneath me.

Jax flopped onto his back beside me without saying a word.

It probably wasn't the time to be drooling over his muscular body, but it was hard not to now that he was within touching distance.

God, he was beautiful.

Maybe that was part of the reason I'd been so speechless once I'd entered his bedroom. Yeah, I'd seen him in a pair of swim trunks, and I'd hyperventilated over his perfect body then, too.

I wasn't sure exactly what was different about those boxer briefs. I suspected it was the way they hugged his body more intimately than any swimsuit *ever* would.

My fingers twitched to reach out and trace every one of those six pack abs, but I didn't. Jax was suddenly less approachable than he'd ever been, and I didn't know how to fix that.

His forearm was resting over his eyes, so I had no clue how he was feeling, or if his expression was still grim.

I need to tell him everything. It doesn't matter whether it's painful for me or not. Jax deserves to know why I had a meltdown on him.

I cleared my throat nervously before I spoke. "I know I told you that I was engaged once. I didn't really want to talk about that because I thought I'd left all that baggage behind me. For the most part, I have, but I think I reacted out of some old insecurities, so I want to tell you about it."

"Tell me," he answered tightly. "I'm listening."

I took a deep breath. "I met Lance in Austin after I got out of the Air Force. I relocated there to do my graduate studies, and I was able to find a good weather analysis job there. He was five years older than me, and was already a practicing architect at a firm in Austin. We'd been dating for eight months when he proposed, and because neither of us were in a big hurry to get married, we decided to just move in together. In hindsight, I probably should have seen the signs that he wasn't faithful, but I think I was too busy with work and school to notice. We'd been together for two years when I came home unexpectedly and caught him in our bed with another woman."

"Jesus, Harlow, it wasn't your—"

"Just let me finish," I interrupted, eager to get through the whole story. "The reason I'd gone home early that night was to tell Lance that I was pregnant. Finding him with another woman turned my whole world upside down. We had a huge argument, and he told me that night that he didn't want *me* or *the baby*. He blamed me for everything. He said I didn't do anything to turn him on, and our sex life was boring, which was why he *had* to cheat. What's really sad is that I probably believed some of what he said was true back then. I was chronically tired because I never got much sleep between work and school. I actually convinced myself that I should have put more effort into the relationship, even when I'd given him all I had to give. Being offered an internship at Montgomery seemed like a good chance for me to start over, so I accepted it. All I wanted was to get the hell out of Austin."

I swiped the tears from my face, angry that even after so many years had passed, that relationship was still such a painful lesson.

I have to keep going. I'm almost done.

"Maybe it was a blessing that I miscarried when I was eight weeks pregnant. It happened right before I moved to San Diego. I don't think my resulting sorrow over it had anything to do with Lance. I fell out of love with him the day I knew he betrayed me, but I felt lost after I miscarried for a long time. I guess I felt like I lost a small piece of myself, even though I'd never planned on getting pregnant," I finished shakily.

Jax hadn't moved, but his muscles were coiled tightly, and the one in his jaw was ticking.

I cleared my throat before I confessed, "After my internship, I dated, but they were nothing more than casual dates. Maybe that's all I really wanted because my ability to trust another man was still shaky." I took a deep breath before I finished, "I haven't been intimate with another guy since Lance. The desire and the attraction just wasn't there for me. Mark and I were still trying to figure things out, so we never slept together, and he didn't push for that. I guess when I made my move earlier, all of those old insecurities about not being good enough came flooding back. I felt ridiculous and rejected. It wasn't your fault, it was mine, Jax. You've never done anything to deserve that, and you've never given me a reason not to trust you. I'm really sorry. I hope you can forgive me, eventually. It would kill me if my past baggage screws up what we have now."

His reaction was lightning fast, and I found myself on my back looking up at him before I could blink.

My heart was racing as his eyes locked with mine from his position above me. Jax's chest was heaving like he'd run a marathon, his body covering mine, and his hands holding my wrists to the bed like he was afraid I'd run away.

The expression on his face was intense, and his eyes were wild as he growled, "I should have grabbed your beautiful ass the second you came into my bedroom. The only fucking reason I didn't is because it was hard to figure out if you were really standing there offering yourself to me. Jesus Christ, Harlow! That's been a fantasy of mine for over two years now. It sure as hell wasn't something I thought would ever play out in reality. I don't know how you can doubt how beautiful you are, but I'd like to kill the bastard who made you feel otherwise."

My heart somersaulted as I realized just how pissed off Jax was on *my* behalf. He wasn't angry because I'd melted down on *him*. He was upset because another man had hurt *me*. "I think my confidence was shaken and I never got all of it back. I know it doesn't make sense, but I panicked, even though my rational mind knows that you're attracted to me. It was my self-esteem that temporarily crumbled because of what happened in the past."

"I get it," Jax said gruffly. "But I *never* want there to be a time when you doubt how much I want you again, Harlow. Maybe I should have made myself perfectly clear a long time ago. Does it help to know that every damn time you walk into a room, my dick gets hard? Guaranteed. Does it help to know that every damn fantasy I have while I'm getting myself off is about you, and has been for a long time? Hell, no other woman can even get my cock hard anymore. Does it help to know that the last week has been both heaven and hell for me? There's nothing I want more than to be with you, but I wasn't sure you were ready for more, for a guy who will *never* get enough of you. Because I promise you, once this starts, you're fucking mine. I will not be able to let you go. If you run away, I'll come after you. So you better make damn sure *I'm* what you want."

Jax's fierceness probably should have terrified the hell out of me, but it didn't. I tugged at my wrists, and he let me go immediately. I took his face between my hands, and stroked my thumbs over his jawline as I answered, "You're everything I want. Why do you think I tried to seduce you? I guess for a few moments, I felt like I was looking at my fantasy, too, and it scared the hell out of me. I crave you, Jax. Every cell in my body craves…you. If I can't get closer to you, it's going to kill me."

I didn't think he really had any idea that he was every woman's fantasy. Billionaire…or not. Montgomery…or not. He was so incredibly hot that I doubted *any* woman could resist him. I knew I couldn't now that I knew the man beneath that mysterious exterior.

Jax didn't just want my body. He wanted…me. All of me. He needed the same intimacy between the two of us that I did. And that knowledge set me free.

I wasn't afraid of the caveman possessiveness inside him. I relished it because I knew it wasn't coming from a place of selfishness or from any kind of need to control me. It was his overwhelming desire to keep me happy and safe.

"Fuck it!" he growled. "That's the only out you're getting, sweetheart."

I wrapped my arms around his neck, savoring the feel of his heated skin. "I don't want an out—"

He cut my words off with his mouth, and I moaned against his lips in relief.

God, it felt like I'd waited forever for this man, and I reveled in the passionate kiss that threatened to overwhelm every one of my senses.

He ravaged.

He cajoled.

He consumed.

And I wanted to do nothing except give him *everything* he was demanding.

This man had given me so much, and everything inside me wanted him to know that I was willing to give just as much.

I wanted his fierceness and his out-of-control desire because that craziness matched my own.

"Oh, God, Jax," I panted when he finally released my mouth. "I need you."

I ran my hands up and down his back, eager to touch every inch of hot bare skin I could find.

My body moved restlessly beneath him, and I released a tormented moan as I lifted my hips, and my core pressed against one very large, very hard cock.

Jax devoured the sensitive skin of my neck, nibbling, kissing, and stroking his tongue over every vulnerable area until I was half out of my mind.

I panted as I threaded my hands into his hair, and tilted my head back, giving him access to any damn thing he wanted.

I wrapped my legs around his waist, straining to get closer to what I needed. "Naked," I gasped. "I want you naked. I have to touch you."

He backed off just long enough to pull the flimsy nightgown over my head and toss it to the floor before he rasped, "If you touch me it's fucking over. Later, baby. I have to see you come."

He tore off his boxer briefs and tossed them on the floor, too, before his body finally covered me, and the two of us were skin-to-skin.

"Oh, God, yes," I whimpered. I'd wanted to be close to Jax like this for so damn long that just the sensation of his hot, smooth skin rubbing against mine was orgasmic.

I was almost disappointed when he lifted his body again, but his mouth was on my breasts before that letdown could fully set in.

"Christ, Harlow," he growled against my nipple. "Every part of you is beautiful."

I moaned as he tormented the stiff peak, and then moved to the other. I *felt* beautiful because Jax made me feel like a sexual goddess. The ferocity of his every touch nearly made me come unglued.

"I need you. Jax..." I mewled.

"I know what you need," he answered, his voice raw with passion, right before he ran his tongue down my belly with an erotic sensuality that made my entire body quiver.

One solid jerk on my panties freed them from body, and my longing reached a fevered pitch as Jax ran his tongue up the inside of my thigh.

I hissed as his palm ran up my other thigh before his fingers became enveloped in the slick heat of my pussy.

Oh, Jesus! I'm not sure I'll live through this!

"Jax," I moaned helplessly. "Please."

"Fuck! You're so damn wet, Harlow," he said roughly. "Do you know how hot it is to feel how much you want me."

Oh, hell yes, I knew. I'd felt the same animalistic satisfaction when I pushed up against his enormous erection.

It was primal gratification that I couldn't really describe.

"Yes," I murmured.

"Do you have any idea how long I've wanted to taste this gorgeous pussy?" he asked as his thumb teased my clit mercilessly.

"No," I panted.

"Yes!" I screamed as his head disappeared between my thighs.

The first touch of Jax's wicked tongue stroking from the bottom to the top of my sensitive flesh sent every nerve in my body into overdrive.

He was merciless as he feasted on my pussy like a madman.

He gorged.

He teased.

He ravaged until my heart felt like it was going to pound out of my chest.

"Jax! Oh, God, it's too much!" I whined, my whole body shaking with a need I'd never experienced before.

My hands tore at the sheets, and my head thrashed as Jax gave me a carnal pleasure that was so staggering I could hardly breathe.

His mouth clamped over my clit, and as it did, I felt my climax start to roll over my body.

It was so powerful that all I could do was spear my hands into Jax's hair and ride it.

"Yes, Jax. Yes!" I screamed, not caring that the sounds of my pleasure were bouncing off the walls of the large room.

My body trembled as it came down from the most earth-shattering orgasm I'd ever had.

I never knew! I never knew it could be like this!

Jax continued to wring every ounce of pleasure he could get out of me before he slid up my body.

I wrapped my arms around his neck and yanked his mouth down to mine, just as hungry to taste him as he was to savor me.

Tasting myself on his tongue as he devoured my mouth was so sensual that I moaned against his lips.

The second he lifted his head, I demanded, "Fuck me. Fuck me right now."

"Condom," he groaned.

"I'm protected and I'm clean."

"I'm clean, too," he rasped, his chest heaving. "Haven't been with anyone for a while now. Only. Wanted. You."

Hearing Jax make that profession tore me apart.

"Then screw the condom," I panted as I wrapped my legs around his waist. "You're mine, Jax Montgomery. You're never going to need a damn condom again. It's just you…and me. And if you ever go, I'll find you, too. I swear I will."

"Fuck!" he cursed. "Having you claim me is the hottest thing I've ever heard. I *am* yours, Harlow. Always will be."

"Yes," I called out in a throaty voice as Jax entered me with one powerful surge of his hips.

Jax was built big, but I relished the way he stretched and filled me. The unholy satisfaction was worth a few seconds of discomfort.

When he groaned, and then started to move, I felt like this moment was a culmination of every carnal desire I'd ever harbored about Jax.

And finally satisfying them was transcendent.

I lifted my hips to every thrust, drowning in the bliss of finally having Jax inside me, around me, part of me.

I love you. I love you so much.

I desperately wanted to scream those words out loud, but I bit them back.

I'd probably been in love with Jax for a while now, but I'd never actually said those words, and he'd never said them to me, either.

I don't want to ruin this moment!

I wasn't about to do anything that might crush the all-consuming gratification that was thrumming through my body right now.

"Come for me, baby," he growled into my ear.

Jax's obsession with making me come made it even more urgent than it already was. I tightened my legs around his waist, and Jax shifted positions until every forceful drive of his cock stimulated my clit.

"Oh, God, Jax, that feels so good," I cried out, the pleasure so intense that I felt like I was going to come apart.

He put a hand under my ass and pummeled into me until I finally imploded.

"Jax!" I screamed, my short fingernails digging into his back because my release was so violent and powerful.

He followed me over the edge with a masculine, throaty groan of release that completely shattered me.

He rolled me on top of him, his hand still on my ass to keep us locked together.

The only sound in the room was our harsh breathing as our heart-rates slowed, and we caught our breath.

I buried my face in his neck, savoring his sweaty, musky scent.

"Worth every fucking minute of suffering," Jax stated gutturally as he stroked a gentle hand through my hair.

I smiled against his hot, moist skin, my body awash in post orgasmic bliss.

His words had summed up *exactly* the way I felt, too.

Chapter 21

Jax

"What in the hell am I doing wrong?" I asked Molly and Tango as I poked at the contents of the frying pan the next morning. "This does *not* look like French toast. Do you guys think this looks edible at all?"

The dogs watched me from their place on the floor on the other side of the kitchen island. Neither one of them looked like they had any answers.

"You guys are no help," I complained as they cocked their heads, and looked at me like I was losing my mind.

Since I was a lousy cook, they probably *did* think seeing me in the kitchen for any length of time was an unusual sight.

I lifted a brow as I looked from Molly to Tango. "I doubt either one of you would eat this shit."

Disgusted, I trashed the contents of the frying pan, determined to try again.

Dammit! I wanted to do something nice for Harlow, and making breakfast had seemed like a good idea when I'd first gotten up. Yeah, it would have been easier to just order something in, but what was the point if I hadn't put the effort in to do it myself?

Leaving Harlow's bed hadn't been easy. When she'd automatically reached out for me in her sleep the moment I'd gotten up, I'd nearly climbed back into her bed.

For Christ's sake, the woman needs to sleep at some point.

We'd spent the entire night sleeping a little...and then fucking. Sleeping a little more...and fucking again.

Harlow would be lucky if she could even walk this morning.

Or should I say this afternoon since it's after twelve?

I'd lost track of how many times I'd reached for Harlow during the night. Finally, in the early morning hours, I'd promised I wasn't touching the poor woman again so she could sleep.

However, when I'd woken up a few hours later to the euphoric sensation of Harlow's beautiful lips wrapped around my cock, that promise had gone south in a hurry.

I'd finally forced myself out of her bed an hour ago so she could sleep, resolute in my decision to make us both breakfast.

We needed to eat after all the energy we'd burned through in a single night.

"Good morning," Harlow said sleepily from the entry to the kitchen. "What are you doing?"

I turned my head, and my heart leapt into my throat as I saw her standing there in the same sexy nightgown she'd been wearing the night before.

I swallowed hard, trying not to remember how quickly that particular nightgown could come off her body. "Entertaining the dogs, I think," I drawled. "Good morning to you, too, gorgeous."

The dogs went to greet her enthusiastically. She fussed over both of them before she stood up straight again.

She shot me a beatific smile, and strolled over to where I was standing. Lifting onto her toes, she laid a good morning kiss on me that made it hard not to drag her back to bed.

Afterward, she eyed the pan on the stove. "Are you...cooking?"

I nodded. "Our French toast came out so bad even the dogs wouldn't eat it."

She laughed, and the musical sound made my damn chest ache.

Harlow put her hand on the handle of the frying pan. "I'll cook if you do coffee."

"I wanted to make *you* breakfast," I said grumpily.

"You have no idea how much I adore you for trying," she answered sweetly. "But I already know it's one of the few skills you *haven't* mastered. I don't mind doing it for you."

"I'm definitely not a cook," I said unhappily as I walked to the coffeepot.

I grabbed one of Harlow's favorites, and dropped the pod into the coffee maker. At least I could operate *that* kitchen appliance.

"It doesn't matter," she said huskily. "You have extremely advanced skills in *other* areas that more than make up for your lack of cooking skills."

I turned to look at her, and then grinned like an idiot when I noticed her eyes were roaming over my body like she'd rather have *me* for breakfast.

I'd pulled on a pair of pajama pants, but I hadn't bothered to get dressed yet.

Well, okay then. If I have a choice, I'd much rather be her stud than her chef.

"You okay?" I asked gruffly. "It was a wild night."

Last night hadn't exactly been a tender night of discovering each other's bodies. It had been more like a raging wildfire that we'd kept trying to put out over and over again.

Immensely satisfying, but totally exhausting.

"I feel fantastic," she assured me as she cracked some eggs into a bowl and started to make our breakfast. "What about you?"

Shit! How could I tell Harlow that she'd rocked my whole damn world last night, and that I'd *never* be the same because of it?

Since I couldn't find a way to convey my emotions in words, I simply said, "Me, too. I'm great." I paused before I added, "I'm sorry about what happened to you in Texas, baby. No woman should ever have to go through that. If you tell me the bastard's name, I'd be happy to have...a talk with him."

Knowing how much he'd hurt Harlow, and then walked away from her when she'd needed him the most, he'd be lucky if he was still breathing when our...discussion was over.

"No, you will not," she scolded. "It was a long time ago, and I don't want you going to prison or getting sued over him. He's not worth it."

I was slightly mollified by the fact that she was worried about *me* and not him. "I think the guy must have had a screw loose to do what he did. Instead of being a dick, he could have supported you and your ambitions. You were working your ass off."

"I'm actually glad he didn't," she replied philosophically as she dipped some bread and laid it gently in the large frying pan. "If he had, I wouldn't be here with you right now. I think it worked out the way it was supposed to be. Maybe previous heartache makes a person appreciate it more when they find a good relationship."

Hell, what could I say about *that* statement? I was damn glad she hadn't married the idiot, too. "It could have been a lot less painful and still ended with you at Montgomery, and the two of us together," I answered as I put cream into Harlow's coffee.

"I may have turned down the internship if I hadn't *wanted* to escape Austin," she mused. "I had a good job, and I could have just sailed through my doctorate. Although, if that relationship had never happened at all, I probably would have applied at Montgomery, eventually. It was and still is my dream job."

"I'd rather it hadn't happened," I told her as I put her coffee down on the island for her. "Did you want the baby, Harlow? Did you have a plan?"

"I'm not sure I really had a solid arrangement all worked out," she said in a thoughtful voice. "I had the resources to raise a child on my own, and I had no plans of giving it up. That was about as far as I got in planning my future. Everything happened so fast. Getting pregnant was completely accidental. I was sick, and I think the antibiotics I got from the urgent care affected the efficacy of my birth control. So it was a shock that led to yet another shock once I found my fiancé in bed with another woman. Everything just compounded until the final blow of miscarrying."

"Did your mother know?" I asked, hoping she had someone with her when it happened.

"No," she said as she shook her head slowly. "Not until after it happened. Because it occurred so early, I was in and out of the hospital in twenty-four hours. There was no point in getting Mom upset. I was on my way back to California anyway."

Jesus! Was there ever going to be a point when Harlow put herself first? "What about *your* need for some support?"

"I got it once I got back here. My mom was there for me," she replied calmly. "I was fine physically. The doctor assured me that I'd done nothing wrong to cause the miscarriage, that they were common in the first trimester, and that there was no reason I couldn't have a child someday."

"But?" I prodded gently.

"But there was still an emptiness that took a while to go away," she responded softly. "Looking back, I'm sure it was grief and sadness after a whole series of shocks, but I *did* get through it, Jax. It just took me a while to trust anyone again."

"Not exactly surprising after what happened," I assured her.

I had to wonder if Harlow had any idea how strong she was, or how amazing it was that she was resilient enough to go through something bad and come out of it without any bitterness.

Her eyes met mine as she said earnestly. "I really am sorry for being an idiot last night. I made peace with that part of my life a long time ago. I didn't know some of those insecurities were still buried. Maybe it would have been different if I'd had an intimate relationship again before we met."

Oh, hell no. I was all good with her having a little meltdown. Thinking about some other guy helping her through her sexual insecurities didn't sit well with me. At all. "You aren't an idiot, and any insecurities you have are fine as long as you talk to me. I can't help you if you don't talk to me."

She shook her head. "You're such an amazing man. I have no idea why some woman hasn't snatched you up by now." She held up a hand. "And don't start trying to tell me all of your faults again. I *know* about all your flaws, and they're nothing compared to all of your good qualities. All of the wonderful things about you were always there, Jax. You just never let anyone see them."

Maybe because no woman has ever wanted to see me. Until Harlow.

"I think I'd be okay with letting you call me a nice guy now," I confessed, wanting to lighten the conversation. "As long as you think I'm hot, too."

She snorted. "I think you're both, and you should know that after last night."

"I do, but a guy likes to hear that shit," I informed her with a grin.

Harlow started dropping perfectly made pieces of French toast onto a plate as she said wryly, "I'll try to make sure that you're always aware of your hotness."

I grinned broader. "You can just show me really often," I offered as I dropped a kiss on her bare shoulder.

"Oh, no, you don't," she said as she pointed her spatula at the full plate. "You're eating right now. Take that plate and move that incredibly perfect body away from me before you get more than you bargained for, mister."

"I think I'd like that," I informed her as I moved her hair and kissed her neck.

"You can like it later," she said sternly. "Eat your food before it gets cold."

"What about you?" I asked as I got out some butter and syrup before I plopped onto one of the stools at the breakfast bar.

"Mine is almost done. Don't wait for me. Eat before it gets cold."

I slathered butter on my French toast, and piled on some syrup.

Harlow took the seat next to me with her plate a few minutes later.

"I'm really excited about volunteering for Last Hope," she told me as she started to eat. "And I'll actually be happy to get back to

Montgomery. Thank you for not accepting my resignation. I would have regretted it later."

I reached for the mug of coffee I'd brewed for myself before Harlow had come downstairs. "I know. That's why Hudson and I didn't accept it. Not to mention the fact that you'd be dangerous if you'd eventually gone to a competitor."

While that wasn't the main reason we'd tried to keep her at Montgomery, it *was* true. Harlow had made some valuable contributions to our company with her research, and she was way too intelligent to be working somewhere else.

"So you just wanted to keep me for my research skills?" she asked jokingly.

"No," I replied honestly. "I think I had my own ulterior motives that I didn't want to admit at the time, but it was a consideration. I wasn't like Hudson and I didn't understand how much you'd been through or that you were making that decision due to guilt."

"When can I go back?" she asked. "I had some important projects happening. I'd like to get back to them."

"When you feel like you can handle it," I said. "You've been through hell, Harlow. Take some time to take care of yourself before you worry about Montgomery."

I had a feeling she'd be back in the lab this afternoon if I let her, and that wasn't going to happen. She'd barely started to take her life back. She wasn't ready for a high pressure job right now.

"I'm better, Jax, and I'm getting bored. I'm not used to being unproductive," she argued.

"Maybe after the holidays," I said noncommittally.

"Are you serious? We're barely beyond Halloween. That's over two months away. Be reasonable, please," she said unhappily.

I thought I was being *very* reasonable. Considering all that Harlow had been through, I actually thought January was too soon.

"That's as reasonable as I'm going to get," I warned her.

I never wanted to see Harlow in the shape she'd been in just a short time ago. If she pushed herself to go back to work too soon, the progress she'd made could easily backslide.

"You're being a tyrant," she grumbled. "Honestly, if I have to stare at the walls of my apartment any longer, I'll lose my mind."

"Then don't," I suggested. "Stay here with me and stare at these walls instead."

Okay, so *that* hadn't been exactly the way I was going to ask her to move in with me, but I guess it worked.

"You'd have the dogs, the pool, the gym, and a lot more space to chill out," I added.

"I can't possibly stay here," she replied. "Jax, we just started a relationship."

"And we can continue it together here," I said. "Don't say *no*, Harlow. Think about it. I'd miss you like crazy if you weren't here. We've been spending every single evening together for a while now. I'd really like to keep it that way."

"The press would have a field day with that," she mumbled.

"They already are," I informed her. "They've seen us go in and out of here all week. Hudson and Cooper have been sending me links to some of the articles. The speculation about our relationship is rampant. That's another reason why I think you should stay here."

I didn't really care what the media thought, but I had to tell Harlow so she was aware.

She groaned. "What are they saying?"

"It depends on what news outlet you look at, but everyone is curious to find out if my dating days are over," I said drily. "The less information they get, the more they make up crazy stories. The last article I saw suggested you were pregnant with my child, and that's why you haven't been seen back in the lab at Montgomery."

"That's ridiculous," she sputtered. "Even if I was pregnant, I could still work."

"Not if I was hiding you away so none of my future conquests would know," I told her with a chuckle.

She snorted. "It's not like you can hold me hostage. That's the silliest bunch of garbage I've ever heard."

"Obviously, you've never seen the I-was-abducted-by-an-alien-and-now-I'm-having-their-love-child type of articles," I teased as I pushed my empty plate back. "I'm generally way too boring to make *those* scandal sheets, but even they have a conspiracy theory now."

She rolled her eyes. "What do we have to do to get off their radar? Those ludicrous stories will get back to my mother, eventually. She hasn't said a thing so far because she's not much for celebrity gossip, and I figured if she did find out, I could just tell her we're dating. But I think the secret baby thing would be a shocker for her."

"We get extremely boring," I suggested. "Maybe like…if we live together and get seen around town once in a while. If we act like a normal couple, they'd be disinterested within a week."

"Jax Montgomery, are you telling me that just to get your way?" she asked suspiciously as she put her fork on her empty plate.

I might be…

Still, the idea *would* work like a charm.

"You did ask how we could get them off our ass," I reminded her. "That would work."

Okay, maybe there *were* other options, like just ignoring them until they went away, but I had to admit, I liked my solution a hell of a lot better.

"Why do I have a feeling you're just picking your favorite fix?" she questioned skeptically.

Shit! This woman knew me way too well.

I wrapped an arm around her waist and pulled her soft, curvy body into my lap. "Because you're way too smart to fall for my bullshit," I said regretfully. "But it would get them to go away, and it would make me a very happy man. Win-win."

"You're shameless," she said with a sigh as she wrapped her arms around my neck.

"You have no idea how depraved I can be when it comes to you," I warned her.

I felt her body quiver as she looked down and our eyes met. "Then show me just how badly behaved you can be," she whispered right before she leaned down and kissed me.

I scooped her body up in the middle of the embrace and headed toward the bedroom without taking my mouth from hers.

Maybe I *was* a lousy cook, but wicked and sinful were definitely my specialties.

Chapter 22

Jax

"It's been five damn weeks, and I still haven't been able to talk Harlow into coming to live with me," I told Hudson and Cooper as the three of us hung out on Hudson's patio. "Every time I bring it up, she tells me she'll think about it. What is there to think about? She packs her stuff, I get it moved to Coronado, and it's done."

Harlow and Taylor were at a baby shower for one of their colleagues at Montgomery, so Cooper and I had grabbed a few pizzas and headed over to Hudson's place. We didn't get a chance to just hang out and have a few beers on a Friday night very often, so we'd taken advantage of the opportunity.

Cooper swallowed a slug of his beer before he said, "I noticed your plan for keeping her off work until after the holidays didn't go so well, either."

Bastard! He would have to bring that up!

"We compromised," I replied. "I'm lucky I got another month from her."

Harlow had just started back to work at Montgomery a week ago.

She'd wanted to go back to work right away.

I'd wanted her to wait until after the holidays.

I'd ended up caving and settling for the beginning of December.

All she'd had to do was accuse me of not trusting her judgment, and I'd really had no choice *but* to negotiate.

"Are you two doing okay?" Hudson asked.

"Yeah," I told him. "Everything is great. I've never been happier in my entire life. I can't say we *never* argue. She's stubborn. But nothing major."

Cooper raised a brow. "*She's* stubborn?"

I let out a long breath. "Okay, we *both* are, but all I want is to see her more often. The house is way too quiet at night when she's not there. Hell, even the dogs are moping."

"It's not like you *don't* see her," Hudson observed.

"She got caught up in work twice this week, and she didn't come over because she left the lab a little late. If we were living together, I'd still see her when she got home." I wasn't about to tell Harlow what to do. Sometimes I had to stay later at the office, too, but it would nice if we still saw each other, even if it was later in the evening.

"I get it," Hudson commiserated. "I guess I'd feel the same way if I didn't see Taylor's smiling face at the end of the day. Why don't you just ask her why she's hesitating?'

I shrugged. "I guess I want it to be *her* decision, and I don't want to pressure her into it. She knows how I feel. I've made it pretty damn obvious."

"I don't really see the point of having a woman around all the time," Cooper grumbled. "Isn't it enough to get laid occasionally and call it good."

"No!" Hudson and I said in unison.

Cooper shook his head. "Both of you are pathetic," he answered disgustedly. "You might as well just jump off the cliff and ask Harlow to marry you—like Hudson did with Taylor."

"I've had the ring in my pocket for three weeks now," I confessed. "If I can't get her to live with me, I hardly think she'll say *yes* to a wedding proposal."

"It is kind of strange that she doesn't even want to talk about you two living together," Hudson said. "She had absolutely no problem making it clear to the reporters that the days of them chasing you on your one-and-done dates were over. Harlow made it pretty evident you two were committed. It was brilliant when she told them that you two liked quiet nights at home with the dogs. By the time she was done, I think all of their eyes were glazed over with boredom."

I snickered. "She knew exactly what to say to make them lose interest. She even offered to let them follow us on a quiet bike ride around the island. All of them politely refused so they could go find a good scandal instead."

Hudson nodded. "The interest doesn't last long when they can't smell any blood in the water. Harlow made your life as a couple sound even more boring than Taylor did."

Harlow and I hadn't needed to worry about being followed around by reporters for weeks now. Not that I was complaining. I'd forgotten how nice it was to go somewhere with a woman and not be hounded by the press. I had Harlow's deft handling of the press to thank for that.

As much as she'd dreaded dealing with them, she'd done a damn good job of getting them off our ass.

Maybe *too good* since she'd had no problem going back to her apartment once they weren't around anymore.

"Be patient, Jax," Hudson advised. "Harlow has always been self-reliant. I have to admit that I was in awe of the way she set up the weather data station at Last Hope Headquarters. Having our info that accurate and precise may have literally saved lives on that rescue two weeks ago. She's a damn good fit for Last Hope."

"I'll ask her to marry me, eventually. I'm just waiting for the right time," I said.

Maybe like... the moment she gives me the slightest clue that she'll accept.

"Great," Cooper said irascibly. "Now I'll have *both* of my brothers acting like they've lost their damn minds all the time."

"Don't be an asshole, Coop," Hudson said as he folded his arms over his chest. "Why don't you finally just tell us what happened with Fiona and stop making all of our lives miserable."

"Nothing happened," he answered stiffly. "It's not that unusual for two people to discover that their relationship isn't working."

"Is that how it happened?" I asked skeptically.

"How else would it happen?" he asked vaguely. "We were just… incompatible."

"And it took you eight or nine months to figure that out?" Hudson pressed. "Come on, Coop. Did she dump you?"

"If you want to put it that way, I suppose so," he mumbled irritably.

"She either did or she didn't," I pointed out. "This isn't one of those gray areas you hate so much."

With Cooper, everything had to have a tidy and logical conclusion.

"She fell in love and married someone else. One of the Appleton heirs, I think. I didn't bother finding out which one," Cooper said drily. "Happy now?"

"Hell, no," I said in a disgusted tone. "Both of the Appleton heirs are total idiots. They were mean little bastards when we were kids, too. Why would she pick one of those pricks over you?"

Honestly, I thought Coop had made a lucky escape. Fiona had been one of those women who wanted nothing more in life than to marry a rich man. She wasn't one of the so-called social elite, but hung out with as many from that circle as possible so she could marry one.

For me, Coop and Fiona had never fit, and I'd never figured out what they talked about when they were together. I'd spoken to Fiona just enough to know that she had zero knowledge on any of Coop's interests. From what I gathered, she used what brains she did have to memorize the names of the richest families in the area.

Still, Cooper had obviously cared about her.

"Hey," I said to Cooper. "I'm sorry, man."

"Me, too," Hudson seconded.

"Nothing to be sorry about," he said tightly. "She wasn't the first woman who decided I wasn't capable of romance, and that I was incredibly boring and uninspired. I've decided that I'm much happier without a relationship in my life."

I didn't want to point out that he didn't sound very damn happy, and he acted like a guy who hadn't gotten laid for over a year. Most likely, he hadn't.

Cooper continued, "I'm glad that committed relationships work for both of you, but I'd prefer to hang onto my sanity and my dignity from now on."

"She never was good enough for you, Coop," I told him. "Don't let a woman like Fiona make you cynical and bitter."

"It wasn't just *her*," he explained tersely. "In case you haven't noticed, I'm not exactly a charming guy. I'm pragmatic and logical, and those qualities appear to be assets that most women *don't* want in a man. I'm not emotional, and I don't lose my mind over any female. It's ridiculous to put emotion over logic."

Spoken like a man who has never found a woman who makes his wisdom and judgment fly out of his brain like he never had any in the first place!

Cooper was a guy who never did anything without carefully calculating the risks and benefits. He was so damn intelligent that the process was automatic for him.

I could see how some women might *perceive* that as being cold, calculating, or unromantic.

What my younger brother needed was a woman intelligent enough to understand how his mind worked. Once she did, it wouldn't be difficult for her to see that underneath all of Cooper's rationality was a guy with a huge heart.

"You'll find the right woman," Hudson told Cooper.

"That would be impossible since I'm not looking," Cooper answered cantankerously.

Hudson chuckled. "That's usually when it happens."

"Everything okay out here?" Taylor asked from the entry to the patio.

I watched as Hudson's eyes lit up at the sight of his fiancée. "Hi, sweetheart, I take it the baby shower is over?"

She nodded. "It is. I don't want to interrupt. I just wanted to let you know I was home."

Taylor walked to Hudson's chair and gave him a brief kiss.

Unwilling to settle for the quick embrace, Hudson snaked his arm around Taylor's waist and pulled her onto his lap as he asked, "Did you have a good time?"

"I did," she answered as she looked at him adoringly. "It's nice to be able to spend time with Harlow in person again. I missed her."

I frowned. "Where is she?"

Taylor turned her gaze to me. "She said she was going home. I invited her to come by tonight because I knew you and Cooper were here, but she said she had something she needed to do."

It's Friday night. What does she have to do that couldn't be done over the weekend?

I got up from my chair. "I think I'll just pass by her place and see if she needs any help. Did everything seem okay with her?" I asked Taylor.

I hadn't seen Harlow since Wednesday, when I'd finally agreed to let *her* take *me* out for dinner. The experience had been both heartwarmingly sweet and slightly uncomfortable, but Harlow had seemed to enjoy splurging.

Hell, that had been two nights ago. I'd been looking forward to seeing her tonight.

If she wasn't coming to me, I'd go to her and help her with... whatever it was she had to do.

Taylor smiled. "She was fine. Harlow looks happier and healthier than I've ever seen her."

Okay, so she'd *cheerfully* decided that she didn't want to see me tonight.

It was comforting to know that Harlow hadn't decided to go straight home because something was *wrong*.

It didn't feel quite so reassuring that she wasn't as eager to see me as I was to see her.

She hadn't called or texted.

She hadn't said anything about being busy tonight.

Then again, we hadn't really made plans, either. We generally didn't have to lay out exactly what we were doing.

Harlow and I always spent our weekends together, so in my mind, something was definitely…off.

I said my goodbyes to everyone, and left Hudson's place not quite sure what kind of welcome I'd get when I got to Harlow's apartment.

Chapter 23

Harlow

"**A**re you okay, honey? You sound a little tired tonight," my mother said in a concerned voice as we chatted on the phone.

I took a sip of my wine. "I'm fine, Mom. It's just been a busy week in the lab."

It felt good to be able to actually talk to her honestly about work again. For a while, I'd had to avoid the topic because I'd never told her I'd resigned from Montgomery.

Luckily, I'd never have to tell her.

It was taking me a while to get back into the flow of working full-time again. After being away from Montgomery for so long, I'd had some catching up to do. I'd done some late nights at the lab so I could clear the backlog, and leave a little more free time to spend with Jax.

"I'm surprised you're not with that handsome man of yours tonight," she teased.

"He's doing some guy time with his brothers. Taylor and I had a baby shower to attend earlier," I explained.

"I'm not trying to rush you or anything, but I wouldn't mind a grandchild or two," she said in a wistful tone.

I nearly spit out my wine. "Mom," I said once I'd swallowed. "We're not getting married. We're just in an exclusive relationship right now."

"You're in love with him, Harlow," my mother said gently. "And it's completely obvious he feels the same way."

I sighed. My parent didn't miss much, so I wasn't surprised that she knew. "I do love him, but we haven't been seeing each other that long. Give us a little time."

"I guess I can wait. It's not like you haven't found the right man this time. I'll get my grandbaby, eventually. Jax is nothing like that other horrible man," she said, sounding relieved.

I smiled because I knew she had a hard time even saying Lance's name.

There was nothing my mother didn't know about that relationship.

"No, he's not," I agreed, knowing she still worried about me, and it had been years since those events had happened. "I'm happy, Mom."

My life was nearly perfect, which was almost frightening sometimes.

I was back into the job of my dreams. I was doing something important as a Last Hope volunteer. Most importantly, I had the most amazing man I'd ever met.

I set my wine down on the table as I heard Molly bark. "I have to go, Mom. Someone is here. I'll see you around lunchtime tomorrow. If he's not busy, I'm sure Jax would like to see you, too. I love you."

"I love you, too, honey," she said before she hung up.

I placed the phone back into the charger, and stood up nervously.

I could hear both of the dogs barking now, so I was assuming that Jax was home.

I can do this. I trust him.

I'd already had my suitcases in the car when Taylor and I had gone to the baby shower.

God, I hope I'm making the right decision. Maybe I should have called and discussed this with him first.

My actions weren't exactly the way I'd planned on letting Jax know that I missed him, and I wanted us to live in the same home.

I was so tired of not seeing him when I got home every night.

But I'd been waiting for something from *him*, and I'd suddenly realized that maybe it was time for *me* to step up, and to *stop* delaying.

Jax had been the first one to make himself vulnerable to me plenty of times in the past.

He was more than worth tossing caution to wind.

To be honest, this wasn't even a risk because I trusted Jax Montgomery completely. The man would do anything to keep me from getting hurt, so I wasn't even sure what had taken me so long.

"Harlow!" he bellowed from the garage door.

Obviously, he'd seen my car outside.

I stopped just inside the kitchen, wondering why he sounded... frantic.

"I'm here," I called as the dogs raced past me.

"Thank fuck!" he cursed as he strode into the kitchen from the laundry room. "I went by your place because you didn't stop at Hudson's after the baby shower. Taylor said you were going home because you had something you needed to do. You didn't answer the door, and there were no lights on in your apartment. You also haven't answered your cell phone. I was getting worried."

My heart melted as I saw the stressed expression on his face.

I threw myself into his arms, and he held me so tightly I could barely breathe.

"I'm sorry," I said contritely as he finally loosened his hold. "I put my phone on the *do not disturb* setting when I got to the baby shower. I usually get bombarded by telemarketers that time of night. I must have forgotten to take it off. I chatted with Mom for a while, but I used your landline. I didn't mean to worry you."

I could feel the tension in his body slowly ebb as he said huskily. "I'm just glad you're okay. You didn't tell me you'd be here."

"It was kind of a surprise," I said carefully.

He grinned. "A very pleasant one for me."

"There's more," I informed him as I motioned toward the other side of the breakfast bar. "I don't plan on leaving this time. Ever."

He looked at the suitcases, and then back at me in surprise. "You're finally moving in?" he asked slowly, almost like he didn't believe it.

I nodded. "I was waiting for you to say something, but I finally realized how ridiculous it was that I couldn't just say it first." I went to him and wrapped my arms around his neck as I looked into his gorgeous eyes. "So, I'm just going to throw my heart out there and say that I love you, Jaxton Montgomery. I love you to a depth I never even thought was possible. My heart is yours forever if you want it."

His arms tightened around me in a powerful grip as he hugged me close to his body. "Jesus, baby," he rasped into my ear. "I hope you already know that I love you. I'm sorry if I never said those words. I should have. I didn't know how damn good it would feel to actually hear you say them."

I shook my head. "I knew, and it wasn't fair for me to expect you to say it first. You show me that you love me every day. You've been there to support me, and I know how important my happiness is to you. I could at least be the one to say the words first."

He pulled back a little so he could search my face. "Hell, if I'd known that all I had to do was say those words to get you here with me, I would have told you a thousand times a day. I didn't want to do anything else to make you feel pressured. I also wanted the final decision of whether or not you wanted to live together to be yours, without me badgering you about it. You've owned my heart since the day I asked you out for dinner over two years ago. I guess I just didn't want to admit that to myself because I knew I was fucked since you obviously weren't interested."

"Oh, I was interested, handsome," I told him playfully. "But even back then, my intuition told me that you could break my heart."

"Never would have happened, beautiful. You already had me by the balls," he said huskily. "Christ! I love you, Harlow. I almost lost it when you weren't at your apartment and you weren't picking up your phone. Don't you know that I wouldn't be able to live without you anymore?"

My heart clenched as I heard the vulnerable note in his tone. "I wouldn't either," I confessed readily. "I want to stay right here with you. I want your handsome face to be the last thing I see every night, and what I wake up to in the morning. I missed you when we weren't together."

I barely got time to finish my sentence before Jax's mouth came down on mine.

Every damn time this man kissed me, my heart exploded with so much love that it was almost painful.

And when he kissed me like *this*, with so much tumultuous passion, I knew there would never be a day when my soul and my body wouldn't respond with the same fierceness.

I wasn't afraid of the crazy way we loved each other.

I reveled in it.

I craved it.

I wallowed in it, immersing myself in a love I'd never even hoped to find.

How could I have known that it even existed before Jax Montgomery burst into my life?

"Jax," I moaned when his mouth went from mine to trail down my neck.

He lingered in the sensitive area right behind my ear, a tender spot that only a very attentive lover could know about.

This man knew every single thing that drove me crazy now, and he used every bit of that knowledge to put me into a frenzy.

I speared my hands into his hair, and ran my nails down his scalp before I finally trailed them down the back of his neck.

"Shit, Harlow," he rasped.

He wasn't the only one who had learned a thing or two.

"I need you, Jax. Please. Fuck me."

I needed to be close to him so desperately that I reached between our bodies and yanked at the buttons on his jeans.

"I got it," he growled. "I'm so damn hard you'll never get them open."

I removed my own, panting with need as I took my panties with the jeans, and tossed them both on the floor.

Jax had his hands on my ass the second I straightened up, and he lifted me effortlessly while I wrapped my legs around his waist.

"Now," I whimpered, wrapping my arms tightly around his neck.

"There's no way I could wait, even if I wanted to, baby," he said in a voice hoarse with desire.

Using the island for support, Jax drove himself home, and I released a moan of relief and satisfaction.

"Fuck! I love the way you're always so damn ready for me," Jax growled as he pulled back and thrust into me again. "Do you know how crazy it makes me?"

"Yes," I panted. "I love it that you want me like this, too."

There was some kind of deep, primal satisfaction in knowing that Jax lusted after me like a madman.

"Harder," I begged as I wrapped my legs tighter around him.

"This hard?" he asked as he pounded into me with a fury that only a man in his physical shape could manage.

"Yes. Oh, God," I screamed.

Jax buried his hand in my hair roughly and pulled my head back so he could devour the bare skin at the side of my neck.

"You're mine, Harlow," he growled against my skin. "You'll always be mine. Say it!"

I arched my back in pure, carnal pleasure. The caveman in Jax made my body hum in satisfaction. "Yours," I panted. "Always. Just like you belong to me."

"Fuck, yeah," he rumbled. "I love you, Harlow."

I clung to him as his hands tightened on my ass, and jerked me to him with every powerful thrust.

"I love you, Jax. So much," I screamed as my climax started to wash over my body.

Jax's mouth came down hard on mine, and I needed that additional connection as much as he did.

I clawed at his back, my body, heart and soul consumed by this man who I loved so desperately.

As soon as he released my lips, I moaned helplessly, completely letting go because I knew Jax would always be there to catch me.

My inner muscles clenched and released violently on Jax's cock as I tumbled over the edge and just kept falling until I felt like I was never going to stop.

"Harlow!" Jax roared as he found his own release. He held my body tight, breaking the fall, just like he always did. "Baby," he said gruffly after we were both spent.

I released the death grip I had on his neck slightly, and laid my head on his shoulder as my heart continued to gallop, and I struggled to catch my breath.

We stayed just like that, tangled together, while Jax buried his face in my hair and rocked our bodies like we were slow dancing to music no one else could hear.

Our hearts knew the notes well, though, and that was all that really mattered.

Chapter 24

Cooper

I t was late by the time I approached the door of Last Hope Headquarters, but I wasn't tired. Since I wasn't a man who required a great deal of sleep, I figured I might as well get some equipment calibrated.

Urgent situations could occur for Last Hope without any advanced warning, so it paid to always be ready.

After Jax had left Hudson's home in Del Mar, I'd stayed for a while to talk to Taylor about her plans to start her doctorate degree.

I liked Taylor.

I liked Harlow, too.

But that didn't mean I could even begin to understand why both of my brothers had completely lost their minds once they'd met those two women.

My two older brothers were brilliant men. How in the hell had well over thirty years of exemplary reasoning ability suddenly left their brains when it came to Taylor and Harlow?

I'd always been perfectly capable of seeing the same woman once or twice a week for months at a time without letting that relationship interfere with any of my regular thought processes.

I gave that woman my attention when we were together, but when we weren't, I didn't obsess over that female all the time.

Honestly, to do something like that would lower my productivity and my brain's problem-solving ability. Not to mention the fact that it was also unhealthy to be *that* fanatical over another person's happiness.

A person was either happy, or they weren't.

I wasn't egotistical enough to believe that I could make a difference in how a woman felt, one way or the other.

The last thing I wanted to do was to put myself into an irrational state by attempting to do something that wasn't even an achievable objective.

Maybe I *had* tried to make a woman happier in her relationship with me in the past, but I'd learned from those mistakes.

I shook my head as I placed my finger on the scanner, and let myself into the building. Hudson and Jax were so far gone that I doubted they were ever going to figure out that trying to make a woman happy was a fruitless endeavor. But since they both seemed perfectly content to keep trying, I'd have to eventually figure out a way to get used to their irrational behavior.

As soon as I entered the headquarters, I knew something wasn't right.

It wasn't just because the lights were already on, because it was possible that Marshall could have forgotten to turn them off when he'd departed earlier.

At first, it was just gut instinct, until I heard someone moving around on the second floor.

Who in the hell would be on the second floor at this time of night?

Marshall's office was there, but his car wasn't, and I knew he'd never be working this late unless we had an urgent case.

He would have called if anything had come up.

I reached behind my back and pulled my small Glock from the holster as I moved quietly up the stairs.

Granted, I didn't know for sure if it was an intruder, but as my mind had searched for the possible identity of whoever was upstairs,

I'd come up empty. There were very few people who had clearance to get into the building, and I knew where all of them were this evening.

No vehicle in the parking lot, either.

So it was very likely that someone *had* broken in.

I stood, with my back against the wall, right outside the small office that seemed to be the source of all of the sounds I'd been hearing from downstairs.

Desk drawers opened and closed like someone was looking for... something.

Since nobody was talking, and I wasn't hearing enough commotion to indicate that there was more than one person inside, I moved quickly.

"Don't move," I growled as I positioned myself at the entrance to the door, and rapidly scanned for my target with my weapon.

The person in front of my gun sight was definitely *nothing* like I'd expected.

One, I'd never anticipated locking onto a chest that had *breasts.*

Two, she didn't look the least bit frightened or intimidated.

Three, the last thing I'd predicted was that I'd get censured by said intruder.

"Oh, for God's sake, put that ridiculous gun away," she said, sounding annoyed. "You'll hurt someone with that thing."

I lowered the Glock slowly. "Who in the hell are you, and why are you here?"

Once the gun was down, I looked the female over, and knew almost immediately that I'd never seen her before.

I never forgot a face, and the woman was so striking that I wasn't sure *anyone* could possibly forget meeting *her.*

Not that she appeared to *try* to draw attention to herself.

She was dressed in a pair of jeans, a baggy university sweatshirt, and a pair of sneakers that did nothing to add to her petite height.

Judging by the wispy bangs on her forehead, her hair was light brown. The remainder of those locks were secured in a thick braid that fell between her shoulder blades.

It's those damn eyes.

Her eyes were a true, rare amber color that seemed to light up her entire face. They weren't a hazel that just resembled the honey colored shade. Whoever this female was, she had eyes with a little melanin and whole lot of lipochrome that made her irises golden. The uniform hue was extremely rare, and almost made her eyes appear to glow.

She let out a sigh as she went back to organizing some equipment on her desk. "I don't know why you'd assume I was here for nefarious purposes. The security in this building is nearly unbreachable, which is why I knew *you* weren't here unauthorized. I heard the door downstairs, and I knew no one could possibly get through that iron fortress without the right fingerprint. My name is Victoria. Marshall just gave me building access earlier today. I couldn't sleep, so I thought I'd come set up the office he gave me."

"There was no vehicle in the parking lot," I said cautiously.

She shrugged. "I parked out front."

"You're really a member of Last Hope?" I put my Glock away as I stared at her in surprise. "How in the hell is that possible?"

She sent me a withering glare as she answered, "I'm not sure why you'd be surprised. I'm not the first female volunteer. I do contract work with the FBI as a linguist. When I started to investigate whether the things I'd heard about Last Hope were real or just rumor, I eventually found Marshall. By that time, I already knew the rumors were true. I offered my services, and he accepted."

I couldn't say that it *wouldn't* be helpful to have a language analyzer and translator available on occasion. However, we did rescues in a lot of different countries. "What language?" I asked.

She sounded as American as I did, so it was hard to judge.

"You mean what *languages*?" Her question was actually a correction. "I speak and write seven different languages fluently, and there are several others that I comprehend well enough to translate verbally. I know the language in every country Last Hope has been to so far, so I think I can be of some help to this organization in the future."

She blinked, and fixed her gaze on me.

There wasn't a single indication that she was bragging or gloating.

In fact, she'd sounded like she was just throwing that information out there to let me know she belonged in this office.

"You even speak Lanian?" I questioned.

Victoria started to rattle off statement after statement in a language I didn't comprehend, but I had to assume it was Lanian.

I held up a hand with a smirk. "Okay. Okay. I got it. So, you're a language expert. I wasn't doubting you. I was just…asking."

I was also impressed and fascinated by someone who could communicate in so many different languages since it wasn't a skill I had myself.

Not only was this woman strikingly pretty, but obviously highly intelligent as well.

Maybe it was the combination of the two that made Victoria so… compelling.

I couldn't remember the last time my dick had gotten hard just from listening to a woman speak a foreign language.

Probably because it had *never* happened before.

I'm sure it's just because I haven't gotten laid for over a year.

Nope. I kind of doubted *that* was the case. I'd seen plenty of attractive females since I'd sworn off dating altogether, and I hadn't had a single problem controlling my dick.

Victoria shrugged. "Learning different languages has always come naturally to me. I was that teenager who always wanted to be a cheerleader, but ended up as the president of the honor society who graduated from high school two years early instead. Pretty much the same thing happened in college, too."

So, she was obviously beyond simply intelligent. I leaned against the doorjamb as I told her, "I get that. I skipped quite a few grades myself. I had a college degree by the time I turned eighteen."

Now why in hell did I need to share that?

She turned her head and smiled at me for the first time.

And…my dick just got even harder.

Against my better judgment, I started to wonder if Victoria might be interested in a fling. It didn't have to be a relationship, right?

"I probably could have skipped more," she explained. "But my parents were worried that I wouldn't have a normal childhood and adolescence if I got too far ahead of other kids my age. That must have been really hard for you to advance so fast. I always felt like an oddball because I was a little younger than my classmates."

"I went to private school," I told her uncomfortably.

"I know," she said as she started to put away some supplies from a small box on her desk. "Judging by your hair color, I'm assuming you're Cooper Montgomery. My brothers talk about you, Hudson, and Jax all the time."

"I am Cooper. Who are your brothers?" She'd totally lost me.

She dropped the empty box into the trash can. "My last name is Durand. My brothers are already volunteers and financial backers for Last Hope. They weren't exactly happy when I dug until I found out the truth. They treat me like I'm still a child sometimes."

Victoria?

Victoria Durand?

Oh, hell no. It wasn't possible that I was this attracted to…

"Don't tell me that you're Torie Durand," I said flatly.

She nodded. "I am. I guess my brothers talk about me to you guys, too."

I saw any opportunity I might have had to get this intriguing woman into my bed swirling down the drain.

"Yeah. They talk about you all the time." I cleared my throat. I wasn't an idiot. I really needed to escape from this situation in a hurry. "Look, I'd better get downstairs and calibrate some equipment. It was nice meeting you, Torie. Maybe I'll see you around." I turned and headed for the stairs.

"Nice meeting you, too, Cooper," she called loud enough for me to hear her.

I groaned once I was down the stairs.

The first woman I'd been attracted to in a long time *had* to be Torie Durand?

Her brothers didn't just *talk* about her; they adored their little sister.

If I so much as touched Torie, the Durand brothers would cut off my balls and shove them down my throat until I choked on them.

We were all friends, and I wasn't actually *afraid* of them, even though I knew how protective they were of Torie. But I respected the way they felt about their little sister since I felt the same way about Riley.

Since I wasn't looking for a relationship, there was no way I was going to mess with the little sister of the guys I called my friends.

Like it or not, Torie Durand was and always would be completely off-limits.

As I got to work, I tried not to think about why that bothered me way more than it should.

Epilogue

Harlow

Two Months Later...

"Happy Valentine's Day, love," I said to Jax with a smile as I handed him a piece of the ice cream cake I'd picked up for him earlier in the day.

He had already given me the best Valentine's Day I'd ever had.

Jax had taken me out for dinner at an amazing restaurant downtown. After we'd arrived back home, we'd exchanged gifts before we'd taken the dogs to the beach for a late-night walk.

I'd pulled out the surprise ice cream cake just a few minutes ago.

He took the large bowl from my hands, and watched as I sat two small paper plates on the floor.

"Now all three of us are spoiled rotten," Jax said happily as he watched Molly and Tango devour the tiny pieces of cake I'd given them, minus the chocolate part.

"You all deserve it," I told him as I sank down next to him on the couch.

"You're not having any?" Jax asked.

I picked up his spoon, took a bite, and then handed the utensil back to him. "I'm still full from dinner, but it's really good."

He leaned forward, kissed me, and licked a tiny smudge of chocolate from the corner of my lips. "Delicious," he agreed in a husky, suggestive tone that sent every single one of my female hormones into attention mode.

That was Jax's I-want-to-fuck-you-right-now voice, and God, how that sexy baritone got me thinking about getting him naked in a matter of seconds.

And he used it really, really often, much to my delight.

I wasn't about to complain that Jax's desire for me only seemed to get more intense as time went by.

Our love grew deeper, and our bond became stronger every single day.

Did we occasionally have disagreements?

Of course we did, but even those squabbles taught us things about each other.

Jax had learned just how highhanded he could be until I pushed back.

And I'd learned what things I could let slide because I loved him, and I knew everything he said and did was out of concern for my wellbeing.

Neither of us fought dirty or mean, and those fights never lasted for very long. We simply respected each other way too much for that to happen. Plus, since the makeup sex was over-the-top amazing, we were usually eager to get to a resolution.

Jax made it a point to find new experiences for both of us to do together as often as possible, but for the most part, we were just happy to…be together.

After a long day at work, there was nothing that made me happier than just hanging out with Jax and the dogs.

I'd finally given up my own apartment, which had made Jax incredibly happy. He'd told me that he'd known from that moment that I was here to stay.

Really? Like I'd actually plan on going anywhere else? Had I known it would please him that much, I would have dumped my apartment immediately. I'd never had any doubts. It had just taken me a while to get everything out of my apartment because I'd been so busy at work.

I couldn't imagine my life without Jax anymore, and it wasn't a scenario I even wanted to contemplate.

"It means a lot that you went out of your way just to get an ice cream cake for me," Jax said gruffly.

I snuggled up to him, and he wrapped his arm around me before he resumed demolishing the enormous piece of cake.

It meant a lot to *me* that he never took *anything* I did for granted.

"There's nothing I wouldn't do to put a smile on your face, handsome," I said earnestly. "I don't want to be the only one who's spoiled in this relationship."

Jax bent over backward to make me happy, and I knew exactly why he did it. I loved seeing his smile and hearing his laughter, too, and I'd cheerfully go out of my way a million times for either one of those things.

He offered me another bite of his dessert, and I shook my head, so Jax polished it off and set the bowl on the coffee table.

"I have one more thing for you, but it's not exactly a Valentine's Day present," he told me as he dug into the pocket of his jeans.

"You promised no more surprise trips for a while after our New Year's in New York City," I reminded him.

That had been a spectacular, magical trip, and my first time flying in Jax's private jet. But I had several important projects in the works at Montgomery right now, so I'd asked him to hold off for just a little while on any spontaneous events that would take me away from work until they were completed.

"It's not a trip," he said, sounding slightly amused.

Okay, so *now* I was curious. Since he'd specified that it *wasn't* a Valentine's gift, it could be anything. Jax Montgomery had no idea how to do surprises in anything other than a very big way. Well, they were always enormous to me, anyway. For him, maybe not so much.

I looked up at him. "What is it? Please tell me it's not another sports car. You're all out of garage spaces, buddy."

That wasn't an exaggeration since all ten of them were now full. The last available spot now housed my Christmas present from Jax, a brand new Porsche 911 Turbo S Cabriolet.

Like I said, he had no idea how to do *anything* in a small way, and I found out that was especially true when it came to Christmas gifts.

My new vehicle could definitely do zero to sixty in under three seconds. However, I'd mostly driven it like a little old lady for the first month or two because I was terrified that I'd scratch the beautiful red exterior. I was starting to relax a little with it now, and I was just starting to really enjoy driving it.

For the most part, I *had* gotten used to Jax's outrageous gifts, but I'd been hoping that I would get a nice long break to recover from the shock of the Porsche.

It would kill me to see the disappointment on his face if I *didn't* accept one of his presents, but that one had tested me mightily.

He grinned at me. "It's not a key to another car."

Thank God!

I accepted the small box with a sigh of relief.

I'd asked Jax if we could just exchange little things for Valentine's Day, and he'd agreed.

Technically, he *had* stuck to that promise, but since I hadn't specified *how many* smaller gifts we could get for each other, I'd gotten an *excessive amount* of presents earlier.

I sighed. Some day I *was* going to finally teach that man that just having *him* was more than enough.

I fingered the small, red velvet box. "Do you want me to open it?"

Usually, Jax's presents were giftwrapped, but this particular box wasn't.

I watched him curiously as he visibly swallowed and then nodded. "Open it."

I smiled and found the catch on the box with my nail that popped the lid open when I pushed it.

Once the contents were revealed, I let out an audible gasp as Jax slipped to the floor next to me, and took my hand.

The hand holding the box was shaking as my eyes met Jax's solemn, purposeful gaze.

"Maybe it's too soon," he said hoarsely. "But I know what I want. I've known for a long time now. I love you, and you're it for me, my once in a lifetime. I wouldn't have a damn clue how to live without you anymore, because you're part of me, and I'm a better man every day because of that. Marry me, Harlow, and I'll feel like the luckiest bastard in the world for the rest of my life."

As he'd said those words, my heart had melted into a puddle at my feet.

Tears of joy were flowing down my cheeks, and I didn't even try to check them.

I hadn't expected this, but did he think for a single second that I'd refuse?

Jaxton Montgomery was my soulmate, and there was never going to be another man I wanted to be with, either.

He was *my* once in a lifetime, too.

I looked at the beautiful ring in my hand. Like everything else Jax did, he'd gone big, and the glittering center stone of the diamond ring looked flawless.

How he'd managed to put so many karats in a ring and *not* make it seem gaudy was beyond my comprehension.

It was exactly what I would have picked out for myself, and I absolutely loved it.

I put my hand behind his head and threaded my fingers into his short locks as I pulled him closer. "Did you honestly think I'd say no to you? I love you, Jax Montgomery, and you're *my* everything, too. So yes, yes, yes, I'll marry you," I murmured right before I put my lips to his.

For once, he let me completely control the embrace. In fact, he barely moved.

I pulled back after the tender kiss and laid my forehead against his. "Are you okay?" I asked softly.

"I think I'm still in shock," he answered huskily.

"Did you really think I'd say *no?*"

He shook his head slightly. "I know you feel the same way I do, but I guess I wasn't prepared for just how damn good it felt to hear you say *yes.*"

My heart squeezed painfully as I pulled back a little to swipe the tears from my face. "Probably as good as it felt to hear you ask me to marry you," I said breathlessly.

There were times I nearly had to pinch myself to actually believe that I was the love of Jax Montgomery's life.

"You could have had almost any woman in the world," I told him. "But you fell in love with me. Sometimes I still find that hard to believe. Never think that I don't feel like the luckiest woman in the world, Jax, because I do. Not because you're obscenely rich, shockingly gorgeous, or carry a famous name. I feel fortunate because a man with a heart as big as yours really…loves me. How could I not feel blessed that I have a man who would very happily put my needs before his own, and has proven that more than once."

Jax swiped a tear from my face with his thumb. "Hey, don't cry, baby. You have and would do the same for me. I think that's what real love is all about. Do you like the ring?"

"It's perfect," I said shakily as he took the box from my hand and removed the ring. "How do you always know exactly what I'd like?"

He shrugged, but he was smiling as he slipped the ring on my finger. "I know *you*, Harlow. I had to stop short of ostentatious, and keep the design classic. I actually had it custom made, but we can make any changes you want."

"I wouldn't change a thing. It's stunning," I told him honestly as I held out my hand to admire the gorgeous ring.

"Just like the woman wearing it," he said as he moved onto the couch and pulled me into his lap.

I straddled him and looked down at his handsome face. "You take my breath away every time I look at you," I told him as we grinned at each other like complete idiots. "You're the most beautiful man I've ever seen."

It wasn't just Jax's perfect body or gorgeous face that moved me.

It was the way I could see his heart in his eyes every time he looked at me.

He shot me a teasing frown. "I hope you see a little bit of the hot stud who can make you come until you beg for mercy, too."

I laughed as I wrapped my arms around his neck. "You know I do. Would you rather I called you my beautiful stud?" I asked.

"Baby, you can call me anything you want now that I know you're going to marry me," he replied.

"You know we'll have to wait until after Hudson and Taylor get married, right?" I pondered. "I want to dedicate my time to her wedding first without being distracted by my own."

"I know. I want that for Hudson, too. Valentine's Day next year?" he asked hopefully.

I nodded slowly. "I think that would be incredibly romantic."

"Let's face it," Jax said. "Your mom probably has most of it planned already. She's already made it perfectly clear that she expects a grandchild or two."

I groaned. "She's pretty transparent on that issue."

He threaded a hand into my hair and pulled my head down gently. "It doesn't really matter to me, Harlow," he said huskily. "A kid or two would be a great bonus, but I already have everything I want right now."

My heart was racing as he pulled my mouth down to his, and gave me a toe-curling kiss that left me panting for more. "I'd like a child or two someday. I love you, Jax," I said breathlessly once he'd released my mouth.

He grasped my ass and pulled me against his massive erection. "Baby, you know what happens when you say that. It makes me fucking crazy," he growled.

Sometimes, *anything* I said made him hard, but I wasn't about to complain about that.

"I bought a sexy little Valentine's nightie for tonight," I whispered beside his ear.

Keeping his hands on my ass, he stood up, and I immediately wrapped my legs around him to keep us balanced.

"Later," he said in a graveled voice. "Anything you put on right now will come back off before I can even get a good look at it. You don't *have* to seduce me, Harlow. It doesn't matter what you're wearing or whether or not you decided to fuss with your hair or put makeup on. You always look like the most beautiful, sexiest woman on the planet to me."

I put my head on his shoulder and tangled a hand into his hair as he strode toward our bedroom.

When Jax said things like that, my heart felt like it was going to explode. I knew what he was really saying was that it was always going to be okay to just be...me. He'd love me where I was, how I was, no questions asked.

"I feel the same way," I murmured.

God knew I'd take this man any way I could get him.

I let out an amused squeak as he tossed me on the bed, and came down on top of me.

I sighed as he buried his hands in my hair and grumbled, "Christ! I love you, Harlow."

As I fell into his exquisite, green-eyed gaze, I said the words back to him, knowing neither one of us could ever hear those words enough.

"Kiss me," I whispered, craving him just like I knew I always would.

When he did, everything was right in my world.

I felt...alive.

I felt...wanted.

I felt...free.

I felt...loved.

I had lost myself for a while, but Jax Montgomery had found me, and he'd shown me exactly what it was like to truly love, and to be loved.

I'd gotten a second chance when I'd walked out of that rebel camp alive.

Somehow, I'd also been lucky enough to find real happiness after absolute despair.

Because I'd experienced both of those extremes, I was absolutely certain that I'd never stop appreciating exactly what I had right now for the rest of my life.

~*The End*~

Please visit me at:
http://www.authorjsscott.com
http://www.facebook.com/authorjsscott

You can write to me at
jsscott_author@hotmail.com

You can also tweet
@AuthorJSScott

Please sign up for my Newsletter for updates,
new releases and exclusive excerpts.

❦————————————————————————————❧

Books by J. S. Scott:

Billionaire Obsession Series

The Billionaire's Obsession~Simon
Heart of the Billionaire
The Billionaire's Salvation
The Billionaire's Game
Billionaire Undone~Travis
Billionaire Unmasked~Jason
Billionaire Untamed~Tate
Billionaire Unbound~Chloe
Billionaire Undaunted~Zane
Billionaire Unknown~Blake
Billionaire Unveiled~Marcus
Billionaire Unloved~Jett
Billionaire Unwed~Zeke
Billionaire Unchallenged~Carter
Billionaire Unattainable~Mason

Billionaire Undercover~Hudson
Billionaire Unexpected~Jax
Billionaire Unnoticed~Cooper
Billionaire Unclaimed~Chase

British Billionaires Series

Tell Me You're Mine
Tell Me I'm Yours
Tell Me This Is Forever

Sinclair Series

The Billionaire's Christmas
No Ordinary Billionaire
The Forbidden Billionaire
The Billionaire's Touch
The Billionaire's Voice
The Billionaire Takes All
The Billionaire's Secret
Only A Millionaire

Accidental Billionaires

Ensnared
Entangled
Enamored
Enchanted
Endeared

Walker Brothers Series

Release
Player
Damaged

The Sentinel Demons

The Sentinel Demons: The Complete Collection
A Dangerous Bargain
A Dangerous Hunger
A Dangerous Fury
A Dangerous Demon King

The Vampire Coalition Series

The Vampire Coalition: The Complete Collection
The Rough Mating of a Vampire (Prelude)
Ethan's Mate
Rory's Mate
Nathan's Mate
Liam's Mate
Daric's Mate

Changeling Encounters Series

Changeling Encounters: The Complete Collection
Mate Of The Werewolf
The Dangers Of Adopting A Werewolf
All I Want For Christmas Is A Werewolf

The Pleasures of His Punishment

The Pleasures of His Punishment: The Complete Collection
The Billionaire Next Door
The Millionaire and the Librarian
Riding with the Cop
Secret Desires of the Counselor
In Trouble with the Boss
Rough Ride with a Cowboy
Rough Day for the Teacher
A Forfeit for a Cowboy

Just what the Doctor Ordered
Wicked Romance of a Vampire

The Curve Collection: Big Girls and Bad Boys Series
The Curve Collection: The Complete Collection
The Curve Ball
The Beast Loves Curves
Curves by Design

Writing as Lane Parker
Dearest Stalker: Part 1
Dearest Stalker: A Complete Collection
A Christmas Dream
A Valentine's Dream
Lost: A Mountain Man Rescue Romance

A Dark Horse Novel w/ Cali MacKay
Bound
Hacked

Taken By A Trillionaire Series
Virgin for the Trillionaire by Ruth Cardello
Virgin for the Prince by J.S. Scott
Virgin to Conquer by Melody Anne
Prince Bryan: Taken By A Trillionaire

Other Titles
Well Played w/Ruth Cardello